"Let's go find her," Griffin said to Ember as he opened his truck door.

The husky jumped in without hesitation and looked back as if to ask what was taking Griffin so long. He climbed in and hit the gas, keeping his eyes peeled as he drove. Bre hadn't known exactly where she'd been run off the road; at least, it hadn't sounded like it from her description. She could have just been in shock. Griffin wouldn't blame her.

But in shock in the dark, cold woods after the day she'd had with someone after her? Griffin hated that. He hated that she was alone.

Something inside him blamed himself, though he tried not to. If he'd told her he'd help her find Addy, would she have been home and safe? Why had she been on the way to his house anyway?

Sarah Varland lives in Alaska with her husband, John, their two boys and their dogs. Her passion for books comes from her mom; her love for suspense comes from her dad, who has spent a career in law enforcement. When she's not writing, she's often found dog mushing, hiking, reading, kayaking, drinking coffee or enjoying other Alaskan adventures with her family.

Books by Sarah Varland

Love Inspired Suspense

Treasure Point Secrets
Tundra Threat
Cold Case Witness
Silent Night Shadows
Perilous Homecoming
Mountain Refuge
Alaskan Hideout
Alaskan Ambush
Alaskan Christmas Cold Case
Alaska Secrets
Alaskan Mountain Attack
Alaskan Mountain Search

Visit the Author Profile page at LoveInspired.com.

ALASKAN MOUNTAIN SEARCH

SARAH VARLAND

LOVE INSPIRED SUSPENSE
INSPIRATIONAL ROMANCE

LOVE INSPIRED® SUSPENSE
INSPIRATIONAL ROMANCE

Recycling programs
for this product may
not exist in your area.

ISBN-13: 978-1-335-58750-3

Alaskan Mountain Search

This is a work of fiction. Names, characters, places and incidents are either the
product of the author's imagination or are used fictitiously. Any resemblance
to actual persons, living or dead, businesses, companies, events or locales is
entirely coincidental.

For questions and comments about the quality of this book, please contact us
at CustomerService@Harlequin.com.

Love Inspired
22 Adelaide St. West, 41st Floor
Toronto, Ontario M5H 4E3, Canada
www.LoveInspired.com

Printed in U.S.A.

My soul, wait thou only upon God;
for my expectation is from him. He only is my rock
and my salvation: he is my defence; I shall not be moved.
—*Psalm* 62:5-6

A lot of people helped to make this book a reality, and I'm so thankful for each of them. Thanks to Greg, my agent, and Carly, my editor, for all the work you did on this story. I appreciate both of you.

Thanks also to Alaska Solstice Search Dogs, especially Vikki, Donna and Stacy. You were so willing to talk to me about search and rescue work with dogs, and it helped so much—thank you! Any mistakes are mine.

Thank you to my high school students, who encouraged me to get this book done. You guys really helped!

And as always, thank you to my family. Whether it's listening to me talk about writing or answering incessant crime scene questions or being patient when we have sandwiches for dinner again, you all contribute to these stories and I'm thankful for you.

And thank You, Jesus.
I love getting to tell stories for You.

ONE

It was never truly dark at this time of year—mid June—in the land of the midnight sun. But as it edged closer to midnight, Bre Dayton could feel the shift in the air that signaled night, the added chill that hadn't been present even an hour before. She could also see the slight dimming of the sun's rays to a tired golden pink that signaled the end of another day.

Another twenty-four hours gone since her seventeen year old niece had disappeared. Thirty-eight hours total now.

"Captain Dayton…" Chief Walker approached, shaking his head as he trailed off.

"We can't give up."

"Not giving up, scaling back."

"We can't do that either."

His look of sympathy was worse than if he'd argued with her, talked down to her, or anything else. Bre flinched away from the pity she saw in his eyes. She didn't want to be the recipient of that pity.

She didn't want her niece to be missing either. Especially not in the vast wilderness of Echo Pass, where four women had died in the past five years. Rumors

abounded around town, though none was strong enough
to deter people from frequenting the hiking trails in
the area. Only some people believed that there was a
serial killer, that the man or woman called "the Echo
Pass Hunter" was real.

Bre believed. She'd seen the evidence, the bloodied
bodies, the senseless loss of life.

The police department knew it was a serial killer
and had called in the FBI after the second woman in
the same general age range—eighteen to thirty—had
disappeared. The discovery of her body and the similar
MO of the killing had confirmed the kind of criminal
they were dealing with.

"What if we split up more so we can cover a larger
area? There may still be a trail somewhere, some kind
of evidence left behind."

"The FBI will still be on the case."

Bre appreciated their help but didn't agree with all
their advice or methods. It was the FBI's advice that had
prevented the Wolf River Police Department from sharing more details about the cases with the public, for fear
of sensationalizing the deaths in a way that made the
killer thirsty for more. Or that caused him—the profilers believed it was likely a man—to change weapons,
as the weapon was one of the only leads the police department had to chase. They needed to do whatever it
took to keep as many people alive as possible. Bre *understood* the FBI's recommendation. But she struggled
with the lack of transparency.

Instead, the WRPD had avoided publicly sharing details about the case but had made it clear that the pass
wasn't safe, that increases in criminal activity were to

be expected; overall, discouraging people from any kind of recreation in that area of the backcountry.

But Alaskans were a stubborn people.

And now Bre's niece, Addy, was the latest person whose life may have been lost because the PD couldn't track down enough evidence to identify this person.

"No one should be walking around here alone. Not with a serial killer loose."

"A serial killer who might have my niece." She faced her boss head-on, not even bothering to keep the anguish from her tone. Speaking the words aloud was almost impossible. Addy *could not* be dead. As Addy's guardian, she'd promised to keep Addy safe, give her the life Bre and Ben hadn't had. The ache in her chest intensified enough that she almost wanted to call on a God she hadn't bothered in years. Hadn't she learned young enough how much good crying out to Him did, as she'd watched the sirens flash the day police had taken her mom away and hauled her and her older brother to a stranger's house?

Once again, the chief didn't speak, but Bre knew what he was thinking. She'd seen the postmortem reports of the women who had died already—at least, the ones they knew about. Most had died within hours of their disappearances. The killer appeared to just materialize, take a victim off the trail, and murder her. The body didn't tend to be well hidden—buried in a shallow grave that too often was disturbed by bears or other animals—but the pass was so remote and untraveled that it was still sometimes years before a victim was found. Maybe if the public knew how brutally these women had been killed, it would be enough to keep people out of the area, but more than likely not. There wasn't a predictable timeline between victims; sometimes he waited over a year, sometimes women were murdered within a few months of each other. In the five years since they'd had their first victim, four women had been killed.

Addy might be the fifth.

Addy should have known better than to hike in the pass alone. Bre wasn't one of those who'd advocated for trying to close the pass completely. Very few people thought that a realistic possibility since it was the center of recreation for the town and encompassed an area over a hundred square miles. But she'd told her niece never go to there alone; a rule she followed for herself as well.

Addy hadn't listened.

Panic pressed at the front of Bre's throat down into her chest. She almost couldn't breathe when she thought about Addy possibly... After all she and her brother had been through, Bre had failed in her last promise to him.

But Bre was desperate. *God...* She tried, but no words came. *Help?* She felt a flicker of something inside, almost like a spark. For so long she'd wanted God to step in and help her, wanted a reason to believe.

Addy did, Bre reminded herself. The teen had been outspoken about it, asked to be taken to church every Sunday, which Bre did whether she'd been up all night working on a case or not, because it was important to her niece. She'd refused Addy's invitations to go inside with her though. People who'd seen what she had, didn't go to church. Or that's what she told herself.

"Bre, are you still listening?"

He hadn't called her "captain," something he was typically very careful to do when they were working—just to make it clear to the people under her command, mostly men, that she was just as deserving of respect as anyone was—but she heard the caring in his voice. This man wasn't just her boss; he was her friend. The man whose wife insisted on fixing her and Addy dinner every Friday night, no matter how much Bre protested that she didn't have to do that. He was almost as invested in finding her niece as she was.

"Sorry, Chief." She blew out a breath, looked out across the brilliant green of the pass. The snow had been late melting this year, but it had melted faster than usual and spring and summer had come in a rush of color so vibrant that it almost hurt her eyes.

It certainly hurt her heart. The world around them was so *alive* and Addy...

"We have to scale back the search. We can't keep going like this."

"Then, like I said, put us in smaller groups to search."

Theirs was already the smallest group, just the two of them and Officer Miller. The others all had four. The chief wasn't taking risks with the serial killer and, while Bre didn't blame him, she was desperate.

The chief continued. "All Wolf River PD is stepping back from is the ground search. The FBI will be handling searches of the pass, and I'll have officers looking into her movements in the days leading up to Addy's disappearance, trying to see if we can establish any links, leads or suspects. If possible, I'll have officers out here canvassing the area, but we can't be all-hands-on-deck anymore. The rest of the town needs policing too."

Arguing wasn't going to do her any good, and Bre didn't necessarily disagree with his decision, except that this was personal. It was *her* niece, her only living family.

Darkness was pressing in further now, the sky changing from pink to a turquoise blue as shadows fell across the mountains.

She exhaled, squeezing her eyes shut. How many people she cared about would she have to let go of?

If there was one thing life had taught Bre so far, it was that people left. Usually by choice. Addy may not have left on purpose, but she was still gone.

A one-word prayer—*please*—seemed to escape from her heart. Even though Bre still wasn't sure she believed anyone was listening, she let it go. She wanted—*needed*—Addy to be okay.

"I need to do one last pass of the area. Please." Bre felt desperation building as time passed. According to postmortem evidence, all the other women who had disappeared in the past, the known victims of the Echo Pass Hunter, had died within twenty-hour hours of disappearing. They were past that already with Addy, and every hour, every minute that passed, made her chances of survival smaller.

Bre could not give up yet. Not even for the day.

The chief considered. Nodded. "I'll come with you. Here's the map. I've marked where we've been so far. Tell me where you want to go and we will go. And then you go home and sleep, understood?"

"I'm not tired."

"It was an order, Captain."

Reluctant, but beaten, Bre nodded and took the map from him.

"Here," she said with more confidence than she felt, remembering the time she'd spent out here in the past. Before the serial killer. The Wolf River Police Department had helped with a search-and-rescue mission. One that had ended in heartbreak in more ways than one.

"This area is thick with alders—" she motioned to the map "—and then, as you gain elevation, there are several areas where someone could hide."

Or where someone could hide a body. Bre might not want to say the words aloud, but she knew they were true. So far there was no predictable pattern to the sites where bodies had been discovered.

"Isn't this near where that missing hiker was buried in the avalanche years ago? You worked that case, didn't you?"

"Yes, it's close. She was just up that way, maybe half a mile or a little more. There are some boulders that signal you're in the debris field from a large avalanche, and then the chute itself is just a little further."

They'd deemed it too risky to recover the body and eyewitnesses—herself and Griffin Knight, a man she'd spent most of the last six years trying to forget—had seen the hiker be swept away by the snow. Bre tried not to think about it. Even with everything she'd seen in her line of work, she never got used to knowing she'd seen someone die.

It had been six years ago… One year before the Echo Pass Hunter had started stalking his victims. If Megan Waverly hadn't died in an avalanche, her disappearance probably would have been linked with the serial killer's spree by now.

Megan had been late to return from a trip across the pass. At the time, traversing from one end to the other, Wilderness Rim to Wolf River, was a popular activity, even for solo hikers. She hadn't returned on time and they'd searched for days before finally finding her a little off the main trail—with the help of Griffin Knight, a search-and-rescue worker, and his Alaskan huskies.

The avalanche had happened before they could make it to her. They'd known it was her, even from the faraway visual, based on what she'd been wearing. The bright orange jacket she'd worn had been enough to visually confirm identity. Questions still nagged at Bre. Why had the hiker been so far from the trail when she was found? She'd been reported as a missing person. If she'd truly being missing, shouldn't they have located her on one of the main trails, trying to find her way back to civilization? Something about it didn't seem quite right to Bre, but without a body, no more investigating could be done, and the avalanche had ruined any hope of recovery.

"Let's go, then," the chief said.

Bre picked up her pace and they moved deeper into the heart of the pass, the quiet of the night around them almost tangible. Bre shivered as she scanned the terrain in front of them and beside them. A chill chased down her neck. From the chill that night had brought? Or from her sense of growing unease? Was someone watching? Was *he* watching?

She could be in a killer's crosshairs right now.

Bre shivered again and this time she knew it wasn't from the weather but from what she knew about the cases. The public was aware there was a serial killer, even if the police department wouldn't say the words. The cops had been working this case quietly for years, together with the FBI, but the public still didn't know exact details. They didn't know why the department referred to him as a hunter. It wasn't for his methodical stalking of his prey, or his distressingly detailed knowledge of this wilderness area. It wasn't for his skill with a gun.

Because the Echo Pass Hunter didn't use a gun. He used a compound bow and hunting arrows. He killed for sport.

And he showed no signs of stopping.

People still hiked Echo Pass because no one ever really thought they'd be next. The path from one end to the other was twenty-six miles. Police had discouraged the pass's use, but Alaskans were a tenacious bunch, and there was no way to enforce any kind of closure, there were too many access points. Besides, with the lack of information, some people probably assumed that the people found dead had perished of natural causes. The Alaskan wilderness cost lives all the time.

The police department had put up trail cameras, but no suspicious activity had been found on them during the last check. Bre knew they'd be checked again now, if they hadn't been already. She'd been too involved in the ground search to know what was going on back at the police department.

The wilderness felt untouched here, unexplored, though they were hiking toward a place Bre had been before. It was the site where one of her dearest friendships had come to an abrupt end after Griffin Knight's willful disappearance from her life. Griffin had been her brother's best friend. A little older than Bre herself, she'd spent what seemed like half her life being fascinated by the man and more than a little attracted to him.

It wasn't just his messy dark brown hair, and the way it seemed to curl at the back and around his ears no matter how much he tried to straighten it. Nor was it his green eyes that had seemed to be laughing at something the entire time they'd been growing up. It was his entire *presence* that attracted her to him. Griffin wore confidence easily, in that quiet way that made her feel like she could relax when she was with him. He knew who he was and owned it. Bre never would have realized how attractive a quality that was until Griffin.

She'd also spent what seemed like half her life running from her feelings. After all, attraction led to relationships, which led, from all indications in her childhood and formative years, to heartache.

But once, six years ago, she'd let herself believe for a little while that falling for Griffin wouldn't leave her alone and heartbroken. They'd been so close to something real while working the search-and-rescue case together. And then the victim had died. Griffin had pulled back, moved to the outskirts of town, and exited her life.

Maybe she could have handled it better if she'd at least kept his friendship. It had meant too much to her to lose.

Bre tried and failed to shove thoughts of Griffin from her mind. His abandonment had disappointed her in ways she couldn't name, ways that made her uncomfortable. She shouldn't have been so affected when he'd left. She'd known better than to let herself depend on someone like that.

Still scanning the area, she noticed no signs of a killer, a victim, or a struggle. Disappointment and relief warred within her. Bre had wanted to look here, just one more place to check, before leaving the pass. On the other hand, not finding a body or signs of one meant that she could hang on to the fragile thread of hope that Addy could still be alive.

"I think we'd better head back." Chief Walker's voice broke into her thoughts. She wanted to argue, she *needed* to find Addy, but the deeper they got into the pass, the more her unease was intensifying. If she walked into some kind of trap, she couldn't do her neice any good. They had to be smart. Her stomach churned and her throat was tight. She only managed to nod.

Darkness blurred the trees, the brush, the mountain edges and the sky. Everything was brushed with twilight and shadows. Bre could feel danger but not see it. She had a flashlight, though it was light enough to see without it, just not light enough to distinguish details. But if she used a flashlight anyone paying attention would know exactly where they were.

If their watcher was the Echo Pass Hunter, it would be as good as painting a target on their backs.

Something in the distance caught her eye.

"Wait." She found her voice, pointed up ahead. "There. That's where the avalanche used to be."

"It melted?" The chief's voice was alert.

"It looks like it. If so, and Megan's body can be recovered, her family could have some closure." Bre tried not to think of Addy as she said it.

"We can look—quickly. Then we go back and bring more people tomorrow. I don't like it out here. Something feels off."

She trusted his instincts, even if she'd worried her own were misfiring and too on edge to be reliable.

"Just a quick look," she promised and hurried up the trail behind him.

They stopped short of the avalanche chute and Bre thought she could make out a body, which looked as though it had been largely preserved by its burial in the snow. It had moved closer to the end of the chute, the riverbed- like dent in the land that had been carved by repeated avalanches, which held tons of heavy snow, than it had been when the avalanche had happened, which made sense. They'd barely been able to see details before.

"Is that…?" The chief's voice trailed off as he reached for his binoculars and held them up.

Wordlessly, he handed them to Bre.

She put them to her eyes and adjusted.

Her attention wasn't on Megan, however. It was on what was sticking out of her.

"Is that an arrow?" she asked in a voice barely above a whisper.

As though her speaking it had brought danger into existence, Bre heard the swoosh of something to her left, looked down and saw a similar arrow planted in the ground. Two, three feet away from her.

"Run!" the chief barked.

Bre sprinted down the trail, back to the shelter of the alders, and dove into the thick cover of the branches, her mind scrambling to make sense of what she'd seen. The arrow had told her what she'd needed to know. Megan had not been the victim of an avalanche. She'd been the first victim of the Echo Pass Hunter. The killer hadn't marked his prey six years ago but he was doing it now.

And now he was shooting at her.

Griffin Knight had resisted getting involved in any kind of SAR effort for more than half a decade, so he didn't know why he'd shown up at the staging area for the search for the missing hiker in Echo Pass.

He hadn't known till he got there who was missing. Addy Dayton. The name had been a punch to the gut. Ben's kid sister.

His best friend had died in a car crash four years before. Drunk driver. He'd gone to the funeral but stayed in the back, far away from Ben's sister, Bre.

Bre Dayton, the single biggest regret of his life… And the reason he was hiking up a mountainside in the middle-of-the-night darkness. He'd stayed out of her way at the search. She probably didn't even know he was there, since he wasn't officially involved. Wolf River Police Department hadn't asked, and he hadn't offered. But he'd spent the last six hours canvassing the area anyway with Ember, his best search dog.

They'd found nothing. He hated that feeling of disappointment but worked to stay positive for the dog's sake. The animals picked up on more human emotions than people sometimes assumed and the last thing he needed was for Ember to get discouraged because of something outside of her control. If there was no trail to find, she couldn't help that.

He'd been heading to his car when a radio nearby had crackled. He'd recognized the voice that said "shots fired" and asked for assistance. Just like he'd recognized the location.

How could one place in such a beautiful mountain pass be the site of so many life moments that haunted him?

Griffin quickened his steps, desperation building inside him. He shouldn't be doing this. He wasn't an official searcher and was certainly not law enforcement. He'd stuck around the staging area just long enough to know that officers were headed up to help, and then he'd started up behind them.

Bre could be hurt. He couldn't leave her alone if she needed help.

The scene was eerie when he reached it. The ava-

lanche chute in the distance where everything had gone
wrong years ago. Closer, officers grouped in a clump
of alders. He hurried toward them even as his mind
took him back.

It wasn't your fault, Griffin. He could still hear Bre's
voice, just like he had in his head for weeks after the
avalanche. Her voice was hot chocolate and a warm
fire. It was more than he'd dreamed of and everything
he hadn't deserved.

She hadn't believed the search-and-rescue mission
gone wrong was his responsibility, but Griffin had
known better. They had remotely triggered the avalanche, unintentionally caused a disturbance that had re-
sulted in the unstable snow releasing and rushing down
the mountain, and he'd been in command. So, yes, it had
been his fault. He'd gone there to save someone and cost
the missing woman, Megan, her life instead. Worse, she
hadn't been just any woman; they had dated, and the
implications from the press had been clear afterward.
There'd been grumblings from those who'd thought he
should have been investigated for murder; not Megan's
family or anyone close to Griffin himself, just random
murmurings of people in town.

Whether Bre had been aware of that before his prior
connection with Megan had emerged in the papers or
not, he'd never known, but it had been part of the reason
for his withdrawal from society. Megan had remained
a friend after their amiable breakup—which had happened because she'd said he clearly had feelings for
someone else.

Bre.

Yeah, maybe he had been in love with her but not
realized it. Since when he was about fifteen. But that

didn't mean anything could ever happen between them. Bre had had too many hurts in her past and Griffin hadn't wanted to be one more of them. He had determined long ago to never contribute to her pain, even if that meant never risking a relationship with her.

He'd broken his unspoken rule—never to let Bre know how he felt—one time. When they were working the search after Megan had gone missing, they'd spent more time together than Griffin could steel himself against. When it had become apparent that his feelings toward her might be reciprocated...

They'd come so close to a real relationship. Instead, all they'd had was one kiss, and then the biggest heartbreak Griffin had ever known.

If she'd felt anything like he had, he'd hurt her worse than he could have imagined, and he hated himself for it. But he couldn't let Bre's future be derailed and, with the rumors swirling around him, he'd worried it would be. How could she move up in the ranks at the police department if the man she was in a relationship with was under suspicion? Besides, he'd felt like a failure, not at all like a man who deserved someone like Bre.

Scientists had confirmed the avalanche had been remotely activated, though they'd been unable to pinpoint exactly where the trigger had taken place, Griffin knew it must have been them. Who else could have been up in the pass at the time? He hadn't seen anyone else but still felt the weight of blame on his shoulders. The avalanche had been an accident. But he should have known better than to take that at face value without examining whether their steps had remotely launched the onslaught. He should have approached from another direction or waited until the snowpack had been more stable. He could have *saved* Megan.

Instead, his recklessness had cost her life.

And cost himself his bond with Bre.

He moved closer to the cops in front of him, unable to make out details in the twilight dark but able to see silhouettes clearly. One of the officers must have heard him approach and looked up. The chief.

"Griffin." The older man looked at him in surprise, moved away from the group of officers.

"Is she okay?" He didn't see any point in pretending Bre wasn't exactly why he was here.

The chief's face was sober, the lines around his eyes heightened by his frown. "She's banged up from diving into the alders. She's not shot, if that's what you're asking."

Griffin felt his shoulders sink, relief flooding through him.

"But…" He tensed again.

"She's not okay, Griffin. She's lost her niece, more than likely, and now the killer is shooting at her. She needs to get out of danger. Work in the office for a bit and let some of my other men and the FBI handle this search, they've sent a handful of agents from the Anchorage field office who are swarming around my department now in their suits."

"She's not going to give up on Addy."

The chief exhaled. "Not likely. And I don't blame her. I wouldn't either. Truth be told, I'm planning to be one of the ones out here canvassing as much as I can. Won't be as often as I'd like, but I'm not giving up, no matter what she thinks."

Griffin nodded, glanced toward Bre again, though he couldn't see her clearly.

"I'll get out of your way," he found himself saying.

"Maybe it's better if you don't."

Heart pounding, Griffin waited. "What do you mean?"

"She could use a friend right now."

They'd stopped being friends when he'd walked away without a goodbye. By the time he'd realized he should have found some way to stay in touch, some way to not become another person who'd left her, it had been too late. The damage had been done.

But maybe…

He could try?

"Just for a couple hours. Hang out with her while she decompresses. That's all I'm asking. Please."

He wasn't asking Griffin to join the search, which was good, because he didn't think he could. He was still skilled in working with dogs, the fact that he was able to run a successful online K-9 training business from his cabin in the woods proved that, but Griffin didn't think he had what it took to be the one out there engaged in another high-profile search with the police.

He blew out a breath. "I'm not sure she'll want to be around me." The honesty hurt, but it was true.

"I just don't want her to be alone. And I need to be here to process *this* scene. He hasn't done this before, and this kind of evidence could help. Besides, I drove her here, and I'd like to her to have a ride home from someone I trust. I don't like how personal this is getting for her."

Griffin nodded. "I'll take her home. If she's willing to go with me."

The crowd of officers was stepping back now and

Griffin watched as one of them helped Bre up. She looked exhausted, but still beautiful. Her dark blonde hair was in a tangle around her shoulders, the curls dusty from taking shelter on the ground earlier. Her petite frame was even smaller than he remembered. She'd always been an entire head shorter than he was, it seemed, but she looked just as strong as ever, her shoulders set back. Nothing about Bre knew how to give up or give in. He'd always admired that about her. She stood now, dusted off the front of her hiking pants. He stayed back, not sure how to approach, and watched.

The chief moved to Bre's side. "You're sure you're okay? I'd feel better if you got checked out."

"I got scratched by some branches and rocks, not shot, Chief. I'm fine."

"At least let me arrange a ride home for you."

"You're not leaving?"

"Not when he's given us another scene to process by shooting at you."

Her face was illuminated by the glow of several officers' headlamps. He watched her consider it then finally nod. "Okay. Find me a ride and I'll go home."

The chief looked up at him.

Griffin swallowed hard, stepped forward, meeting her dark brown eyes, "Hey, Bre. It's been a while."

TWO

He hadn't expected her to be thrilled to see him, but even Griffin had underestimated just how unwelcome his presence would be.

"What are you doing here?" Her face had gone even paler than usual, and her brown eyes stood out. They were red-rimmed, the dark circles speaking for themselves of how much she'd been putting into this search.

What did he say to that?

Something inside him nudged. *The truth.* But telling Bre he still cared about her wasn't on the table. Instead, he took a deep breath. "At the moment, giving you a ride home."

She looked to her boss and Griffin thought he saw the flickers of fight in her eyes before she evidently thought better of it. "I'll be back in the morning."

The chief nodded. "As long as you sleep first. See me at the station before you come out here."

Bre nodded and started back on the trail. Griffin stood still for a second then moved after her, Ember on the leash beside him.

"You'd think she could have at least said hi to you," he commented to the dog under his breath. Ember turned and gave him a look, her pale blue eyes almost seeming to see right through him. Yeah, Ember was definitely on Bre's side, judging by her facial expression. Must be a girl thing.

Bre was moving quickly down the trail, despite the darkness of the hour, like she'd memorized the gentle rises and falls of the path. She never stumbled. And wasn't that like Bre? Her steadiness was something he'd always admired about her, but sometimes he wondered… Did she know it was okay if she wasn't perfect all the time? If she let that put-together façade slip?

"My truck is this way," he said to her when they reached the parking lot.

"Same one?"

"Still works fine." He shrugged. The black F-150 was nearing twenty years old, but still dependable.

Bre almost smiled at that. Once upon a time, he'd been able to make her smile without effort. He'd taken that for granted back then.

They started driving toward town.

"What were you really doing there?" He saw her shift in the seat to face him as she asked.

"Looking for Addy."

In the seat beside him, she was silent for a heartbeat. "I didn't think you'd care."

"That's a ridiculous thing to say. Ben was my best friend."

"Some friend. You weren't even at his funeral. Do you hate me that much?"

"I was there. In the back. I didn't want to bother you." He tightened his grip on the wheel and counted down the miles to her house. Three miles. Another minute. Two miles. One mile. This was why he'd left town and stayed up in his cabin like some kind of modern-day hermit. People had too many expectations, and if you hurt them, the guilt tore at you. Dogs were much easier to get along with, so he'd taken his group of Alaskan huskies, trained both to mush, and work search and rescue, sometimes simultaneously, and just disappeared from society, for the most part. His cabin was only five miles outside town, but it was enough. He rarely left the property, except to hike or train his dogs. His trips to town were few and far between.

They pulled into Bre's driveway.

"And I could never hate you," he finally said, glancing her at he put the truck in Park. "I'm sincerely sorry you think that. I'm sorry I just left." The apology wasn't half the apology she deserved but being in such close proximity to her after all these years made it hard to think, to do anything other than feel. It felt *right*, being with her, and for the life of him, Griffin couldn't imagine how he'd gone this long without her being a daily part of his existence.

For half a second, he thought she might forgive him for stepping out of her life without a word, but then she blinked and the moment was broken.

"Thank you for the ride at least."

"Are you sure you don't want a ride to the clinic? I'm happy to drive you there if you want."

"I'm sure. But…" Her words trailed off and she looked back at him. "If you want to help… I could use a partner tomorrow to search the pass. There's no way the chief is going to let me go on my own, and I'm sure he feels like he doesn't have the manpower. Besides, you have Ember…"

"No."

"Five minutes ago you wanted to help and now it's an immediate no? No consideration at all?"

"It's not like that."

"What is it like then, Griffin? Tell me, because I never have understood."

She was meeting his eyes again now, raw emotion chasing across her face.

"I'm not sure I can help…"

"Did you hear about Megan?"

He actually flinched at the woman's name, the memories Bre had dragged up so casually. Accident or not, he felt responsible. He should have done a better job.

"The Echo Pass Hunter shot her, Griffin."

"She was killed in the avalanche. I *saw* her." He felt his jaw clench, fought against his mind which wanted to replay the nightmarish scene again as it had so many times. Some kind of trauma response, he would guess, but not one he had done anything about besides try to ignore. In the old days he'd have talked to God about it, but he hadn't even done that.

Bre was shaking her head. "No. The Echo Pass Hunter shot her with an arrow just like he's shot every other woman who has gone missing in that pass. She must have been his first victim. Not a victim of what you view as your carelessness. It was not your fault."

His breath caught in his throat and he swallowed hard, feeling his pulse quicken as he fought too many emotions to name. It was like nothing he'd ever experienced, hearing that something that had defined his life for years was a lie. He had assumed it had been his fault, since he was likely the one who had triggered the avalanche. A desperate desire to believe her, to allow that relief to sink into him, warred against his own self-doubt.

"How did you find that out?"

"That's what we discovered tonight. We were searching for Addy up there, and the snow has melted and there she was…"

Her family would appreciate the closure, Griffin thought, though the knowledge that she'd been murdered would be something else to deal with.

But not his fault…. He blew out a breath, then inhaled again. Maybe his first full breath in six years.

"Please help me find Addy. She's honestly all I've got." Her voice broke and he watched her swallow hard, her jaw tense as every muscle in her face refused to let her cry.

And if Griffin let her down again? If he couldn't find Addy?

"I haven't done a search in years. I'm a dog trainer now, not a SAR team member anymore." The last thing he wanted to do was refuse her, but no matter what she thought, he knew he wasn't the right man for the job.

"Yet you were out there today searching."

Dabbling in it. Trying to see if maybe…maybe he could still do some good. But he and Ember hadn't found anything.

"It's better if I don't. I'm sorry. I'll give you the numbers of some of the people I used to work with, though. A couple don't live far from here, just over in Wilderness Rim. They'd probably be willing to help."

"But I want you. To help me, I mean. Please, Griffin."

He could *not* let her down again. That meant refusing no matter how much he wanted to take the risk and help her. "No. I can't, I'm sorry. I can't risk being the one to let you down like that. And even more than that—" he caught himself quickly, stunned at the personal admission that had come from his lips "—Addy's life is too important to trust to my rusty search-and-rescue skills. You need someone else. Please."

She said nothing. Just sat there, petting Ember. Breathing. Then finally she shook her head and let herself out of the truck.

"I really thought maybe I could count on you." Her insinuation was clear as her eyes flashed their anger at him and she shook her head, slammed the truck door and went inside.

Griffin sat in the driveway, petting Ember's head and ears until he saw lights turn on in the house so that he knew she was safe. At least, relatively so.

Had he really said that to her, about not being the one to let her down?

It was true, though. He wasn't good enough at SAR work anymore for Bre to put her hopes in. He'd done the right thing in turning her down, even though it was killing him to know that he'd disappointed her. Hopefully one day she'd see that it was better to be a little disappointed now than crushed later if she'd trusted him with such a big job and he hadn't come through.

And if she read too much into what he'd said, how he'd refused, then she'd realize he still cared and…then what? He wasn't in a place to have a relationship, definitely not with her after how he messed it all up so badly the last time. Griffin needed to do a better job keeping a lid on his feelings or getting rid of them altogether.

It was long past time to move on. But if his relationship with Megan had taught him anything, it was that he might never be over Bre Dayton.

He didn't see that changing anytime soon.

No amount of tossing and turning was going to help Bre get any sleep, not tonight. Her niece was missing, possibly dead, bleeding in a mountain pass somewhere, and it made her want to crumple. But Bre couldn't. Wouldn't. And the only man she'd ever loved wouldn't help her when she was asking.

Bre hated asking for help; did Griffin not realize that? She wouldn't have done so at all if it weren't for Addy. And for Ben, whom she had never been able to stand letting down.

She rolled over again, the pillow warm underneath her head, then sat up and turned it over to the cool side. A deep sigh escaped her lips and she let herself think about Ben. Only for a minute, she promised.

Ben was every bit the larger-than-life older brother that every little girl dreamed of having. Her protector, her friend. He'd been the one constant in a childhood that had lacked many. They'd stayed close as adults, even when Ben had made decisions Bre hadn't agreed with—like marrying Addy's mom, Jen. The woman had left her baby with Ben and run off to chase a life that made her happier. Bre wasn't sure what kind of life meant abandoning a husband and a baby, but Jen must not have found it. She'd died after overdosing on drugs when Addy was four.

History repeated itself in some very uncomfortable ways. Their mom had overdosed in Bre's senior year of high school. Bre and Ben been living with a foster family by then, so it hadn't impacted Bre as much, or so she figured. Ben had done his best to shield her even among the court hearings, the shuffling, the packing up her trash bags with her belongings and moving homes for the third time in a week. They'd never known their dad, never really had a functional family since their mom had been high or drunk more often than not.

But Ben? He'd been the best brother she could have asked for. He'd taken her to the park, pushed her on the swings, helped her figure out how to braid her hair when all the other girls in her class had started showing up for school with cute braids their moms had done for them the night before. He had done everything he could to fill the gaps their parents had left.

And then he'd died.

And no one had been there to cushion that for Bre.

She'd always thought she'd had Griffin to rely on, too. That though he wasn't her brother—she'd *never* been able to think of Griffin as a brother, no matter how much she'd tried when she was a teen. No, a brother never would have made her stomach flutter when he smiled at her the way Griffin did. She'd spent way too much time wondering what kind of girls he was interested in, wondering if she could ever be that. There may have even been a bit of doodling on her notebook involving their names in middle school that she'd carefully kept hidden from him. But while she'd assumed her crush wouldn't last, that one day her heart would move on, she'd thought Griffin would still always be there.

Funny how wrong you could be about someone.

The Griffin from tonight cared in some way; she knew he did. But he was willing to do nothing while her niece needed him, and that wasn't something he could reconcile with the man he'd been. No sooner had the thought formed than she thought of how he'd been after the avalanche, the failed SAR mission. It had changed him, wrecked him.

She knew what it was like to feel like you'd been destroyed and then have to find a way to carry on. Maybe that was why as hurt as she was by Griffin, she couldn't find it in her heart to be angry with him. Not really.

She wasn't going to be able to sleep tonight. Bre threw back her covers and glanced down at her choice of PJs. Sweatpants and a long-sleeved T-shirt was decent enough for her mission.

Lying her in bed regretting the past and feeling sorry for herself for being alone wasn't going to find Addy. But there was a chance, however small, that Griffin would still agree to help her. No matter how much Bre hated asking for help, she would do anything for her niece. If that meant driving to Griffin's cabin in the middle of the night and invading his privacy to beg for him to change his answer, that's exactly what she'd do.

At the front door, she hesitated for a second, her hand already poised in front of the handle. Thoughts of her own safety, the danger she might be walking into, were quickly eclipsed by thoughts of Addy. Addy was worth whatever risks she had to take.

She unlocked the car and climbed into it, taking a deep breath to steel herself against her nerves. It wasn't like her to be afraid. Getting shot at earlier had shaken her up, she decided as she backed out of her driveway and turned the car in the direction of Griffin's place.

The serial killer had seen her tonight. That thought hadn't quite sunken in, and Bre wasn't sure she wanted it to. He knew who she was, had been close enough to almost hit her. Had the miss been intentional? Some kind of warning?

She thought of Megan's body, the arrow in the middle of her back. That spoke of someone skilled with their aim. Megan had almost certainly been the Echo Pass Hunter's first victim.

Why hadn't Bre been his most recent tonight?

Immediately, she heard Addy's voice in her head, telling Bre if she had experienced something like that, it was God's providence, His hand at work, keeping her safe, whether she believed or not.

Some part of her heart softened, thinking about her niece's deep faith, nurtured by Ben, and then she remembered that all that faith hadn't stopped Addy from being taken, maybe tortured, even killed. How could God allow such evil in the world?

Bre had seen so much that she couldn't unsee. Belief that Someone had the power to stop it and didn't... She just couldn't wrap her mind around that.

The miles went by quickly and soon she was at the base of Disappointment Peak. The irony struck her as almost funny, that this was where Griffin had chosen to build his little cabin and hole up, away from the world. What had he been disappointed with? she wondered. With life? With her?

She was gaining elevation quickly, navigating the hairpin turns of the switchbacks with her hands tight on the wheel, sweat making them slick.

She'd only driven here once before, years ago when Griffin had first left town for the cabin. She'd made it all the way to his driveway, prepared her speech; the one where she admitted that she loved him and probably always had. She'd gotten the car door halfway open and then imagined what it would be like if he said he didn't feel the same. He'd already left her once, but if he'd left her *again*, if someone else she'd cared about abandoned her one more time, she hadn't been sure she could take it. So she'd left him. Let him have the life he'd chosen away from her and everyone, and she'd not been back up the mountain since. The drive had been terrible then, and not just because of her nerves. The guardrail had always struck her as woefully inadequate, the curves harrowing.

If she'd thought those things had been concerning in the daytime, they were even more so at night. By the time she realized she should turn around and try again when it was light, it was too late.

Then she noticed the headlights behind her. Not too concerning, except that it was almost three in the morning. Try as she might to come up with legitimate reasons why someone else might be on the road, Bre couldn't think of any. She tensed up.

The car came closer, following on her tail so closely that if she hit the brakes, she'd wreck.

Bre felt her pulse speed up. She pressed her foot a little harder on the gas.

So did the driver behind her. One more hard acceleration and she felt the impact of the vehicle ramming into her. The force whipped her head forward then slammed it back again as she fought to stay in control.

Someone was following her to Griffin's house.

That meant either they knew where Griffin lived and had been waiting, watching, for her... Or they'd known where she lived and had been lingering.

Neither option was comforting.

Her phone was in the cup holder, the ringer turned

up loud on the off chance that Addy would call to tell her everything was okay. That she'd left her car at Echo Creek Pass but, really, she'd been somewhere safe, and that she was sorry to have made Bre worry. That she wasn't lying dead in the open air, she was fine.

Addy hadn't called. Her silence spoke loudly, and Bre didn't want to hear it.

And now this. Could she make a call to Griffin and warn him? Ask him to call 9-1-1? Would this guy go to Griffin after he did whatever it was he was planning to do to Bre? Or was she the only target?

The arrow from earlier was fresh in her mind. Her heart pounded harder and her throat tightened.

She should call work to let them know there was a threat against her. She should…

Another impact juddered her car and made it skid. Bre screamed. She couldn't take her hands off the wheel to call anyone, not like this, and she didn't feel like she even had enough focus to use the Bluetooth features. Talking to anyone would distract her from what she was doing, and could prove deadly. She accelerated hard, going as fast as she dared around the hairpin turns, willing herself to ignore the edge of the mountain. Her only chance at this point was to outdrive her pursuer. Her defensive driving training had largely sat unused in the back of her mind until now; Wolf River wasn't exactly an urban metropolis with bold drivers trying to elude police. Her skills were admittedly rusty.

The noise of a revving engine built in her ears as she caught movement out of the corner of her left eye. The car swung around her, cutting her off and Bre jerked the wheel hard to the right as she hit the brakes. Her SUV impacted the guardrail but kept going, rolling one rotation…two… Bre lost count in the dizzying flips as she tried to stay calm, breathe.

The other vehicle came to a stop on the road above and Bre unbuckled. She had to get away from that driver. Whoever had hit her had been willing to take huge risks in order to take her out. The Echo Pass Hunter? Someone else who had Addy? Completely unrelated?

Regardless, her training and instinct both told her she needed to disappear, quickly, before anyone found her and finished the job they'd started.

Her head throbbed with a deep ache, and she felt what must be blood trickle down her forehead, but she grabbed her phone and moved away from the cars as hurriedly as she could. The darkness was ever so slightly lighter than it had been when she'd left her house, but it was still twilight. It was light enough to see, though in the thickness of the trees it was dark enough to offer her some protection from anyone who might be pursing her. At least, Bre hoped it would. She swallowed hard against the bitter taste of fear in her mouth and moved through the woods. When she was far enough from the car to feel somewhat safe, she pulled her phone out to send a text to Griffin, relieved to see she still had service. She hadn't thought to grab her SAT phone. Bre breathed deeply as she typed out the text. She didn't dare call, in case the killer had followed her and her voice gave away her position.

Text WRPD and tell them I was run off the road. I'm somewhere on the side of Disappointment Peak, on the road that leads to your cabin. Not far from the ski area.

A text came back almost immediately, the phone buzzing in her hand. She tightened her grip around the phone to muffle the noise, listening for any signs that someone had followed her.

What?? Are you okay? I'll come find you.

If she was right and the person who ran her off the road wanted to make sure she was out of the picture, then they'd be coming after her soon. That meant Griffin could put himself straight in their crosshairs if he set off on some kind of ill-advised rescue mission. Besides, she'd gotten herself into this mess. Asking him to help her for Addy's sake was one thing. Asking for herself was another, and Bre wasn't going there.

No. Stay where you are. Just call the police please. I'm afraid to call in case someone is following me and hears me.

Bre paused, lifting her head up. Something had caught her attention, a sensation of not being alone, an awareness that someone else was nearby. Chills crawled up her spine.

I have to go, she typed out quickly. I think they're coming after me. The subtle noises in the woods seemed to confirm it. Bre could picture him, if it was the same person who'd tried to kill her earlier. Indistinguishable build and face, since she didn't know who it was, but holding a compound bow, aiming an arrow straight at her... Her phone vibrated and she glanced down one more time.

I'll find you.

Griffin might not want to be the hero he'd been once, or might not feel like he'd ever been that person, but he just couldn't shake his innate goodness, could he? It was just as much a part of who he was as his gruff exterior or his affection for animals, especially dogs. Bre slid the phone into the pocket of her hiking pants and continued moving through the woods, going deeper as she did so.

She wasn't far from a local ski trail that was used for mountain biking in the summer. Moving on established trails would be easier than picking her way through the woods, and even more importantly, that getting to those paths would give her a location where she could ask for backup to be sent. But there was added risk. She didn't want to be found by the wrong person.

The ski trails would have to wait. Right now she needed to get herself as deep into the darkness of the woods as possible, find somewhere to wait out the last bit of night, and pray that when morning came she could find her way to safety.

THREE

"Let's go find her," Griffin said to Ember as he opened his truck door. The husky jumped in without hesitation and looked back as if to ask what was taking Griffin so long. He climbed in and hit the gas, keeping his eyes peeled as he drove, not feeling any hesitation within him either. It seemed that in the moment, he had enough confidence to believe they'd get the job done. This was what they did; they found people. Bre had given him a fairly good description of where she was, even if she hadn't known exactly where she'd been run off the road. He wondered if her texts were short because she knew she needed to hide, or because she was going into some sort of shock. Griffin would understand either way.

But in shock in the dark, cold woods after the day she'd had, with someone after her? Griffin hated that. He hated that she was alone.

Something inside him blamed himself, though he tried not to. If he'd told her he'd help her find Addy, would she have been home and safe? Why had she been on the way to his house anyway?

He knew the answer, he admitted to himself as he navigated the road. Bre wasn't one to give up easily. More than once he'd let himself wonder what it would be like to be counted as one of those people; thought about how it would feel to be worthy of that kind of single-minded focus. Some people went through hardships and it made them hard. But every single thing Bre had been through had only made her more beautiful to him, more capable of love. Griffin was sure he didn't know every detail about hers and Ben's childhood, but he knew enough. Probably more than Bre realized.

He knew enough that he shouldn't have told her no. Even though he was convinced she'd be better off with someone else helping her, he should have told her yes. Then she'd be safe.

Unless he messed up again. Like he tended to do.

Griffin flexed his hands on the wheel. He couldn't let her down. It just wasn't an option. Somehow, he'd be enough this time.

Not for anything romantic. He knew he'd messed up there, and Bre didn't do second chances with people who hurt her.

But he would do his best to help her tonight and to find Addy.

"Think you can handle one more search-and-rescue mission? Just one." He glanced over at Ember. Her wise, warm eyes asked questions he didn't have answers for. The K-9 had always been able to read him, or at least it seemed that way to Griffin.

Ember was the smartest dog he knew. And he'd need every bit of that intelligence, the almost uncanny intuition she sometimes seemed to possess. When he mushed his huskies, Ember was his lead dog; able to anticipate the trail ahead and what was best for her team and her musher. When he'd taken on a search-

and-rescue mission, she'd been his right hand, his eyes, ears, and definitely his nose. He'd trusted his life to her hands—paws—many times, and she'd never let him down.

His truck headlights caught something up ahead, and it didn't take long for Griffin to see the damaged guardrail where Bre had had go through and over onto the side of the mountain and into the woods. He started ticking items on his mental list, mind starting to detach from his emotions the way it did when he led a search. The way it *had*, he corrected himself. That wasn't his life anymore. This was a onetime thing, to make sure Bre was okay now and to find her niece. Then he'd…what? Disappear back into the woods once again and try to forget all the ways his life might have been different—just maybe—if he'd been willing to take a chance?

Focus. He had to focus. Griffin pulled the truck off to the side of the road, shut off the engine, and snapped Ember's search vest on. Even at times like this, when they weren't officially searching, he liked to use it as a cue to help her understand what he was expecting and what her job was. Immediately, Ember's eyes seemed to spark as her focus sharpened.

"Good girl. We're going to find her, right?"

She stuck her head under his hand and he petted her then opened his door. "Ember, search." He didn't have a scent item to give her to hunt for Bre specifically, which meant she would find anyone who was in the woods.

Immediately, she headed into the woods, her paws making almost no sound on the forest floor. Griffin hurried to follow, thankful again for his choice to use huskies in search and rescue. At first, it had been a matter of convenience. He'd already owned huskies as a dog musher when he'd first had the opportunity to train in SAR work, so he'd chosen to train the dogs he already had, thanks to the help of several talented friends who had showed him how while he was still learning himself. But after using them on searches and comparing them to other K-9 breeds, he felt like huskies moved more naturally through the wilderness, with less noise. It wasn't often necessary; most searches didn't involve likely criminals who were also pursuing the missing person, but it was useful if he was doing a search like and needed to not be noticed.

Maybe it was because huskies had more of their ancestors' instincts than some newer breeds of dogs. Griffin didn't know, but he appreciated it. He watched Ember lift her nose slightly in the air, reading her body language for cues. Her shoulders tensed in a way that made him think she had Bre's scent. The dog stilled then turned abruptly toward the right. Griffin followed.

He dodged long branches of spruce trees and hurried to keep up, stepping over roots on the forest floor. There was more light than there had been when he'd left his house, but it was still dark enough he wished he could use a headlamp. But with someone out here potentially after Bre, he wasn't willing to risk drawing attention to himself and possibly leading her pursuer right to her. She was in enough danger as it was.

That was something he didn't need to let his mind focus on. Someone was *after* Bre. Wanted her dead. It would take all his self-control not to ask Bre to please just hole up somewhere safe and let other people look for Addy. Not because she wasn't capable—she was the most capable person he knew—but because he just didn't want her hurt.

* * *

Out here alone, on the damp ground underneath a spruce tree, Bre couldn't decide if the coming daylight was a blessing or not. On one hand, she would welcome the warmth of the sun. She hadn't taken the time to dress appropriately for leaving the house. How many times had she told Addy that it didn't matter how warm it was outside, she *always* needed to have a jacket with her in the car *just in case*. She was wishing now that she'd listened to her own advice. She wasn't cold enough to be in danger, but the night air wasn't warm and she wasn't comfortable. To make matters worse, she'd worked up a sweat during her initial flight; now that she had slowed down, it cooled on her skin.

She'd only ceased running maybe five minutes ago, deciding she was likely far enough away that stopping was a good idea. Bre feared that if she walked around for too long, she would be in danger of ending up back where she'd started and putting herself into even more danger. Staying put seemed smart for now.

She toyed with the idea of sending a pin of her location to Griffin. Then he could find her even faster. But though it seemed unlikely, she was uncomfortable sending her direct location over the phone. Did she think the Echo Pass Hunter was screening her messages somehow? No, not really… But neither could she rule it out. If she was here for too long, if it felt like she needed an immediate rescue, maybe…but right now it felt like too much risk, farfetched as her concerns might be.

Was Griffin really coming, like he'd said he would? Or was she waiting for police officers to rescue her? She was torn between wanting Griffin to come himself, but fearing he'd back out again, and needing to hope that someone else cared and wouldn't let her disappear out here either to foul play or the wilderness itself.

All her life she'd had a crush on him but it had been easy to dismiss initially. Of *course* she would have a crush on her brother's best friend; it was almost a rite of passage. But Griffin was too good to be true in so many ways. He came from a family with parents who loved him and his siblings. They'd gone on family vacations, and camped, and made s'mores around a fire in the summers while Bre and Ben had tried to figure out how to patch holes in sheetrock after their mom's latest deadbeat boyfriend kicked holes into their living room wall. It didn't make Bre feel unworthy of him, it concerned her that he wouldn't be able to understand where she'd come from, maybe not be able to understand her. And didn't everyone want to fall in love with someone who not only loved them back for who they thought they were, but who they *really* were?

Worse, what if he did understand? What if his friendship with Ben had enlightened him enough that he was able to really know her...and then she still wasn't enough for him? Surely she wouldn't be able to be the chocolate chip cookie baking wife he probably hoped to have one day. Maybe that was why he'd been able to walk away from what they had. Maybe he'd suspected she would never be who he really wanted.

When they'd worked together on Megan's disappearance, she'd started to believe the attraction—the *whatever-it-was*, because it seemed like more and stronger—wasn't one-sided. They'd danced around the subject of maybe going on a date as they'd pursued Megan's trail, and started spending more time together outside of work. Then one night he'd kissed her and Bre had known in that moment that she couldn't hide her heart from him any longer. She loved him. And it was real, not a crush.

Then he'd walked out of her life within a week. She should have seen it coming. That was her fault.

And yet? She blamed Griffin too. While she didn't like people giving her sympathy because of her past, shouldn't he have understood that she would take his disappearance from her life even more personally? Like maybe start to think it was something about *her* that made people disappear?

Then Ben had died.

Now Addy was missing.

Not everyone chose to leave. But Bre admitted she did seem to have a more difficult time than most hanging on to the people she loved.

Loved. Because yes, she still loved Griffin. But she would never let him know. They'd had their chance, and nothing had come of it. She wouldn't take that risk again. Even if Griffin changed his mind one day and wanted to try again at whatever they had been starting, she would turn him down. She wasn't going to wait around for a man. Some people just weren't meant for the settled life, and Bre was pretty sure she was one of them.

She exhaled and leaned back against the base of the tree.

The snap of a branch made her come to attention. She jerked her head up, eyes widening as she scanned the forest around her. It was still twilight but edging toward the first light of morning. The limbs of trees further away from her were dark against the medium blue of everything else. She could make out limbs, shadows, dense forest, but no details.

Another snap.

This wasn't a normal forest noise. She'd had enough training to know to pay attention and to listen to the sounds around her, to analyze how they made her react.

These noises sounded like fear.

Human. Not Griffin.

And getting closer.

Almost unconsciously, Bre slowed her breathing and closed her eyes. There was the temptation to pray again, but this time she abandoned it. Changing her mind and risking a prayer for Addy's sake was one thing, but for herself it was another.

If she died tonight, would someone else search for Addy like she was? Bre thought it unlikely, unless Griffin changed his mind. For so many reasons, dying wasn't an option.

She sat still, barely breathing for what felt like an hour, but was probably five minutes, maybe ten. She didn't hear any more noises, and she had a sense that whoever was nearby was waiting, hoping she'd make a mistake.

This was an individual, she realized, who had a deep knowledge of the backcountry. A true woodsman. That made sense, given the fact that the person after her was likely the Echo Pass Hunter. The FBI had worked up a profile, and wilderness skills was something they'd assumed he had in some capacity. But Bre suspected they'd underestimated him. He didn't just have wilderness skills; he almost became a part of the vastness of Alaska. That must be how he was able to eliminate his victims so easily.

She knew he was close now. Too close. But rather than

pursue her, he was lying in wait. She felt like prey, and hated the feeling.

Finally, she heard the faintest hint of footsteps on the forest floor, moving away from her. She didn't dare move, in case it was some kind of trap, but she allowed her shoulders to relax slightly. And she realized she'd changed her mind. Bre was hoping Griffin would come find her. More than anything right now, she wanted to not be alone.

Frustration was building inside, and Griffin was trying not to let it get the best of him. He could tell Ember was feeling similarly, and he didn't know if she was picking up on his own emotions, or if she was bothered by the fact that their search had been fruitless thus far. Breathing deep, he tried to calm the pounding rhythm of his heart, to slow his breathing, in the hope that the rest of his body would take the cue and release some of the tension it was holding. And that, in turn, Ember would relax.

He was watching the dog closely, so he noticed almost the instant the husky's body language changed. It wasn't an alert, not one to celebrate. Rather it was an awareness that he hadn't noticed in her until now. What else—or even more terrifying of a prospect, *who* else—did she smell?

Taking his cue from her, he slowed his body movements and tried to notice the details a dog might notice. The ground was damp from the light rain that had fallen earlier, but not enough for him to make out tracks. Was the area near Ember more pressed down than where they'd been before? Ember was sniffing at it like she'd picked up someone's scent. From her behavior, it wasn't

Bre's. She seemed on edge, uneasy. In his experience with search dogs, they were trainable and alerted to specific things that they were told to find, but they were also creatures with their own minds. This smell made Ember uneasy, and Griffin trusted his dog.

He had to find Bre. Quickly. Every minute that passed was another one she was in danger, and this time, it was Griffin's fault, no matter what anyone said. He didn't want to be responsible for leading a search when he didn't feel like he could do the best job. Addy mattered to him too much for that, and so did Bre. But what good had refusing done him? Bre was out in the middle of the night for who knew what reason, probably to come to his house to tell him all the reasons why he should have changed his mind, and now *she* was missing.

Ember let out a low growl and looked off into the distance.

"Ember, come." He whispered it, but she heard. Obeyed, even though her body language told him she didn't appreciate being called off.

Bre was his focus right now.

God, we need Your help. She's out here, but knowing that doesn't do me any good if we can't find her.

He prayed easily, even as he felt another flicker of conviction that he didn't relate to God as deeply as he once had. He believed, he prayed, but he held some part of him back now, which he hadn't fully realized until today.

"Come on, Ember. Search." He worked to refocus the K-9 on the task, ignoring the unease in his gut that anything had pulled her away from her search. Ember was the best search dog he had for one reason—she was smart enough to know when not to listen to him. It was also what made her a good mush leader. She knew her commands, knew how to do what was asked of her, but in situations where that wasn't the best course of action, Ember had the brains to redirect and do what needed to be done. The fact that she had been sufficiently distracted by something to forget the search? Griffin didn't like that.

Ember left the troubling scent behind and took off toward the left, still moving more quietly than seemed possible. He followed her. When he rounded the next corner, he saw her under a tree next to…

His mind registered human clothes and the human form as he braced himself. This was the part that gave him nightmares at night; that made him never want to search again. It was the question that constantly haunted him. Would the next person they found still be alive? Or would it be too late?

Griffin hated when he was too late. It had happened very few times in his search-and-rescue career but even one time had been one time too many.

"Griffin!" Bre's whisper. His shoulders sank with relief. She was alive.

Not too late this time.

FOUR

"Bre. You're okay." Griffin knelt on the ground beside her and pulled her close to him. "Are you okay, are you hurt?" Exhaling, he released her and moved away. For the second she'd been in his arms she'd felt safe, warm, like she wasn't alone. Now she was colder than she had been.

He'd been so eager to put space between them. But if he wanted distance between them, why had he pulled her to him in the first place?

"I'm fine."

He was still right beside her, only not touching her at all.

"Don't leave. Please." She couldn't be alone right now. Even the thought him standing and walking away with her behind him was too much for her at the moment. After the last several hours, she wanted someone by her side.

If she were honest, she wanted Griffin's arms wrapped around her like they had been a few seconds ago but with him not letting go, maybe telling her that it was going to be okay.

"I'm not leaving. But we need to get out of here. It isn't safe."

His voice left no room for argument, and one reminder of the danger still surrounding her was all Bre needed to find the strength to stand. He was right.

She took a deep breath and steeled herself against what was sure to be an exhausting hike out of the woods. If they made it out.

Her heart had just started to pound, a panic response she recognized but felt powerless to stop, when Griffin reached out and took her hand. His hand was warm, solid, and full of the confidence she presently lacked. He squeezed once. And Bre returned it.

It didn't mean anything, she knew. Not to Griffin. And yet it was what Bre needed right now, just something to make her feel less alone, like it wasn't her against the world, against Addy's kidnapper and her pursuer.

They made their way back through the woods, finally catching site of the road and Griffn's truck, and Bre tried to stop shaking.

While she sat in the truck and shivered, Griffin checked the truck over, even lying underneath it—checking, Bre knew, for any kind of tampering that could have been intended to kill them—before finally coming inside and starting the engine. It started easily, no additional drama.

"I think you may have seen too many crime shows." Bre attempted to tease him, but with her voice quivering from the cold and the stress, the effort at being lighthearted fell flat.

"I'm not taking any chances with your safety."

"Besides refusing to help Addy," she said between shivers.

He looked at her for a long minute.

"That wasn't fair," she finally said. "I'm sorry." And

she was. Yes, she was upset he had refused to help her search, but hadn't he just spent all night out in the woods with a possible serial killer to find her?

The truth was that Bre didn't know how to feel about Griffin, or how to feel when she was around him. He tangled up her emotions. Or did she do that herself?

"You okay?" he asked her.

Bre shrugged. "I'm fine."

He started driving, away from his house, and Bre assumed that he was going to bring her car over in the morning. Wait, her car had wrecked. She'd have to call someone to tow it. She felt her body tensing more and more as they approached her little neighborhood. Being alone did not sound appealing right now, but it was four in the morning; it wasn't as though there were a lot of other options for places to go. But if her pursuer had followed her toward Griffin's…had he been watching Bre's house? Did he know where she lived?

She shivered harder.

When he bypassed her neighborhood, she frowned and turned to him for an explanation.

"You need to see a doctor."

"I'm fine." As long as you didn't count the soreness from earlier in the night and the fact that she couldn't seem to warm up, even with truck heater cranked as high as it went.

"You're stubborn."

She opened her mouth to argue and shut it immediately when she realized it would only prove his point. Judging by the smile tugging at the edges of his mouth, he had realized that too. Bre frowned. "Fine. You can take me to the doctor."

Five minutes later, they were pulling into the small

local hospital and Bre raised her eyebrows. "I'm not *that* hurt."

"No, but nothing else is open this early and I'd feel better if you were checked out sooner rather than later."

She nodded and let out a sigh. Everything was suddenly catching up to her and she felt like she'd been run over and left on the side of the road. It was a good thing there wasn't anything romantic between her and Griffin anymore, if there ever had been, because Bre was sure he wouldn't be attracted to her not at her best right now. It was better this way, that they were just sort-of friends, like they'd always been, the last five years excepted.

Not that Griffin had ever made her feel like she had to do anything special with her appearance. Right before everything had ended, he'd once told her that she was beautiful. She'd been searching all day, her hair in a ponytail, blond wisps escaping around her face, and he'd said she was beautiful.

Maybe she did need to be checked out by a doctor. She wasn't usually this sentimental. Bre felt weak, vulnerable in so many ways, and she hated it.

She reached for the door and opened it, then turned back to Griffin. "Thanks for bringing me."

"Where are you going?"

"Inside. To see the doctor. Like you wanted."

"Not waiting for me?"

"You're staying?"

The brief look of hurt that passed across his face was deep and then, just as quickly it was gone, replaced by the neutral mask she felt like he wore so often. What did he think? What did he *feel*? These were things she'd wondered before and not always gotten answers to. He'd never been much of an open book and that was part of what attracted her to him. But Bre also felt like it was hard to build a relationship with someone who wouldn't tell you what they were thinking.

Again, she remembered how quickly he'd let her go after pulling her into his embrace when he'd first found her. Maybe he wouldn't disclose his feelings to her because he didn't want them to get too close.

"You need a ride home."

Despite the urge to argue with him and say she could take care of herself, Bre exhaled and nodded. "I do. Thanks. I appreciate it."

Maybe all he could give her right now was his presence. Part of her wanted more; part of her had always wished for his love. But this was better than losing him. At least she wasn't entirely alone.

Griffin nodded and they both started toward the Emergency Room entrance. Being out in the open made Bre tense her shoulders. It was an indefensible position, and she didn't like it.

How long, she wondered as she entered the ER, until whoever was chasing her succeeded? And had they already succeeded in harming her niece?

Griffin hated doctors' offices. They were too bright, too sterile. The antithesis of the outdoors, where natural light grew and faded with the time of day, and dirt was everywhere. This wasn't his element, but he hadn't wanted to leave Bre alone.

She'd thought he would leave, even when she might be hurt and was definitely in danger. It bothered him. It probably bothered him even more than he'd thought it would.

He was looking down, trying to read some outdoors

magazine, which struck him as a ridiculous concept. Did people really read magazines about the outdoors, rather than go out and be in them?

"That's quite the frown."

Bre's soft voice immediately relaxed him, and Griffin almost couldn't breathe for a second at the surprise of learning that. Years of living alone out in the woods, trying to find some semblance of peace, and all he'd needed was Bre? That would be cruel irony.

"Just thinking."

She nodded, not asking what about, which he appreciated. "Ready to go?" he asked as he stood, trying to find his balance in the conversation.

"Yes. I'm dehydrated, so they gave me fluids. I was only mildly hypothermic, but they did their best to warm me up. I should be fine." She shrugged. "See? I told you I was okay."

She had told him. But Griffin hadn't been willing to risk her safety.

Wasn't he risking Addy's safety, though, by refusing to help search for her? Bre would certainly say so.

"I thought I'd take you up to my house to get your car and then you can stay and have breakfast with me, or head home. Whichever you prefer."

She nodded, and they headed for his truck.

"Did you call the police when I was in the woods?" She turned to him, her face alarmed.

"Yes, what's wrong?"

"I need to call. I can't believe I forgot to call." She pulled her phone out. Griffin did his best to focus on his driving so she could have at least a semi-private conversation, but it was hard not to hear at least her side when they were sitting a foot away from each other.

"I'm fine… No evidence I saw but feel free to send a team out. Thought of that, yes. I'm not staying away from my own house. No. Okay. Going to Griffin's now. He has my car. I'm not sure actually. Thanks, Chief. I'll call later."

She hung up and turned to Griffin. "They're going to investigate the crash site and see what they can find. Thanks for calling them the first time. Also, why is my car at your house?"

"I had it towed. It's got some damage from where you hit the guardrail, but nothing too serious. More cosmetic than functional, it sounded like, from talking to the mechanic who looked it over when it was towed."

"Why are you being so helpful?" she finally asked after a minute of silence.

"Why wouldn't I be?"

Her eyebrows quirked. "You told me no yesterday when I asked for your help. Now you just keep helping me when I request it. Finding me in the woods. Rescuing me. Taking me to the hospital. Now the car towing? I don't get it, Griffin. Help me get it."

"I'm not trying to avoid helping you. That's not why I said no to helping you search for Addy." Had she paid attention to his words then at all?

"You said no immediately."

"I told you my skills are too rusty. I don't want you putting your trust in me. Addy deserves the best searching for her. And that's not me any longer."

Ember shoved her way forward from the backseat, nosing his arm, as though she took offense to that statement. Ember might be the best there was, but even the best search dog needed a partner and Griffin wasn't sure how much of a partner he was capable of being anymore.

"I'm going to be doing it alone if you won't help."

"That's your choice, I told you who else to call. People I trust."

"Well, I trust *you*, Griffin!"

Neither of them spoke for a while after that. The muted road noise through the closed windows of the F-150 and the hum of the engine were the only sounds.

"Maybe you shouldn't."

More silence. What else was there to say? Just when he figured she'd given up on any further conversation, she spoke again, her voice soft but insistent.

"I just… I don't understand how you can treat me like you do, hold my hand when I'm cold and scared, and then…"

Abandon her. He heard the unspoken words and knew that her past must still be haunting her more than he realized.

Was that was he was doing? Abandoning her?

If he helped her, though, and things went wrong…

She must have seen the shadows on his face because, when he looked over, she was shaking her head. "I'm sorry. I wouldn't ask you if I felt like I had any other options. But I guess I shouldn't ask you anyway. You're not obligated to me in any way. You've done more than you should have already. We aren't really…we haven't… it's not like we've been super close and now you're leaving me on my own for this. This was always my fight, so…" She trailed off. He couldn't remember seeing Bre look defeated before. Not even when he'd seen her at the funeral after her brother died.

"I thought we were close." The words were out before he could edit them.

"We *were*." It sounded so past tense when she said it.

It felt like a standoff, the kind no one could win. Griffin didn't know what to say. Winning could hurt Bre. Losing, giving in and helping, could hurt Bre.

Ember sighed in the backseat. Not for the first time, he wished she could talk. Even without that, though, he noticed something important about himself. He hadn't told her no today, to searching for Addy. Not really. He had told her why he shouldn't, why someone else was a better option.

But there was a possibility he was willing to let himself be talked into helping. *Please*, he begged God, *don't let this be a mistake. Don't let anyone else die because of me.* He felt his faith flicker to life, something beyond the cordial faith he'd had the last few years. He could feel his relationship with God.

"I just don't want to let you down," he finally admitted as he pulled into his driveway and put the truck in Park, taking a deep breath, feeling his heart pound. "I care about you too much for that. I wish—"

"Stop."

He looked up at her. She was shaking her head. "Don't say anything else, Griffin. We were friends once, and I'd like to be again. Let's not mess that up."

Shot down before he'd even hardly started to tell her his true feelings. "Yeah, you're right." He hoped his voice sounded half normal and nodded. "About Addy. I don't think I'm the man you need…to help you search…" He cleared his throat. "But if that's what you want, I'll do it."

Because whether she wanted to hear it or not, he'd realized he could—and would—do just about anything for her.

FIVE

After Bre had told Griffin she definitely still wanted his help, he'd suggested they go in so he could make her breakfast and she could tell him what she had in mind for the search. Everything inside her was still recovering from driving past the site of last night's wreck. She'd gotten a pit in her stomach when she'd seen it again. There wasn't much visible evidence, but the bent and twisted guardrail had drawn her eyes like a magnet down into the trees below and she'd remembered rolling, the sounds of crunching metal, the taste of fear in her mouth. It had been tempting to haul Ember up to the front seat and twine her fingers in the dog's comforting fur, but she hadn't been sure the huge husky would appreciate being hauled around. Instead she'd taken a deep breath and reminded herself that some of her fellow officers would be by the scene soon to process it for evidence.

Then, when they'd driven far enough down the road that she'd started to let go of the physical tension she was holding in her body, they'd gotten to Griffin's house and he'd started to tell her…what?

She'd cut him off before he could really say, but it had

sounded enough like a confession of his feelings for her that she'd panicked and refused to listen. It served her right that she was curious now, her anxiety still churning in her stomach. She should have listened to him, at least been kinder than she had been, but she hadn't wanted to hear anything she couldn't unhear.

He said they were friends and thought they were close. That didn't fit with how Bre had felt when he'd left town without hardly a goodbye. She didn't know how she was supposed to take that as anything but a reflection of how little their relationship had apparently mattered to him then.

Still, the smell of coffee brewing and sausage cooking on the stove for her seemed to demonstrate that he cared, at least some. Or he might just be being courteous by cooking for two. Maybe she should have let him say what he'd wanted to, but Bre couldn't risk his declaration being something more than that. If there was anything she'd realized in the last few hours of being reacquainted with Griffin, it was that she couldn't afford to hand him her heart again. This time, they wouldn't even approach the line that divided *friends* from *more than friends*.

The smell of the sausage had brought another dog into the room.

"Who is this?" Bre asked, reaching for the blond dog.

"That's Flapjack."

Bre reached for his ears and started scratching behind him. He leaned against her, soaking up the attention. "How many do you have?"

"The two that live inside. They're my primary search dogs. I have four more who live outside and mush."

"He's adorable." She looked up at him and smiled.

"Thanks. Also for breakfast…scrambled eggs okay?" he asked, his brown eyes warm.

Bre nodded. Swallowed hard. It was going to be more difficult to keep her heart in line than she'd hoped, as was evidenced by the flutter inside when he looked at her, but surely she was stronger than some little flutters. After all, she was well practiced in ignoring attraction. There'd been a couple of men here and there who'd asked her out over the last few years, after Griffin. But that kind of heartbreak didn't lend itself to trusting again, so she'd turned them down.

Besides, none of them had ever caught her attention the way Griffin had. She didn't want some half strength version of romance. If she was ever going to have it, she wanted the real thing.

For her, that had always been Griffin.

"Scrambled eggs." She had to repeat what he'd asked to bring herself back to the present conversation and out of a train of thought that would do her no good. "Yes, please." Bre reached down to pet Ember, who was sitting beside her, but the dog felt tense under hands. She frowned. "Does she usually stare out the window like that?"

Griffin looked away from the stove in her direction. "Only if there's something out there. Could be a rabbit. We've had a lot of wild rabbits around here the last couple of years. Or a moose."

Or whoever was after her. Bre didn't need him to voice the unspoken thought.

"I'm not too concerned right now," he said even as he moved to the window and looked out, then let the blinds down. Casually. Slowly. As though he wasn't trying to destroy line of sight from anyone who could be out there with a gun and ready to fire if she stood in front of the window in the right place and presented them with a target. Though the man she feared typically hunted with arrows, she wasn't willing to bet her life on him not using another weapon if it proved necessary.

The Echo Pass Hunter was starting to haunt her every waking moment. That and, without Addy, the hollow ache in her stomach were the only predictable companions of her waking hours these days.

Ember did stop staring when Griffin shut the blinds, so Bre felt a little comfort there. Griffin might try to make her feel better or sugarcoat the danger, but dogs did no such thing. They were honest—what you saw was what you got—and they never held their feelings back to protect yours.

Maybe she should get a dog. She'd toyed with the idea when she'd first moved out on her own, years before, but had decided she didn't want the added responsibility. Now it seemed like it might be worth it, if she could get a dog as dependable as Ember. Besides, Addy would enjoy having a dog. And Addy was coming home at the end of this. She had to be.

"You don't have to protect me, you know."

Griffin looked at her like she'd lost her mind.

"I m-mean…" She stuttered a little at the look of utter disbelief on his face, the implication that not protecting her wasn't an option. She could refuse to cross any lines romantically and still appreciate that fierce protectiveness, couldn't she? What was a little wholehearted devotion between friends? "I didn't mean literally. Please, if someone comes after me, feel free to stop him." She laughed nervously. "But you don't have to protect me from the truth. I know someone might be out there who wants me dead. You don't have to shut the windows and tell me it's okay. I'm not a little kid anymore."

"You're not."

He'd said the words, but did he believe them? They'd first met when Bre was eleven, when she and Ben had moved into a foster home next door to Griffin's family. Griffin and Ben had been fast friends. A year older than she, the two of them had frequently left her in the dust for their own adventures, but she'd managed to tag along sometimes. Was that how he saw her still? Was that the real reason he'd broken up with her?

And how much did he know about her childhood? Did he know about all the times Ben had hidden her in the back of a closet when they were really little, and told her the yelling and crashing noises of her parents fighting and throwing things were just from the TV?

"Thank you." She held her head a little higher.

Griffin set plates down and then came around the counter to sit beside her. He bowed his head for a couple of seconds before he ate, and Bre assumed he must be praying. Had he prayed before? She didn't remember him being especially religious, though she knew he'd gone to church as a kid, and it was strange to her to see him praying, believing now. How could adults believe in something that sounded like a fairy tale? She wouldn't have thought he would. But people changed. Or so some said. If she really believed that, wouldn't she be willing to give him another chance, ask him what he'd wanted to say earlier?

He took a bite of eggs and followed it with a swig of orange juice, then looked over at her. "So," he started, "what did you have in mind?"

A very-much-uninvited image the two of them scooting closer and kissing popped into her mind and Bre blinked it away, still trying to figure out what he was asking. Because it sure wasn't *that*.

"About the search," he clarified, almost seeming to read her mind, like he'd always been able to do. "Where did you want to start, or how did you picture me helping?"

Even before Megan's death, when they'd worked together briefly on a couple disappearance cases that had been easily solved, Bre had noticed that Griffin was extremely humble about his talents as a search-and-rescue K-9 handler. He would talk up Ember all day long, but he hadn't seemed to realize how his intuition, the way he'd worked with his dog, and his attention to detail had all helped in the search. It was just how Griffin was, unaware of how good he was at what he did.

But he wasn't asking for a pep talk right now. And Bre certainly wasn't about to give one.

"We canvassed the pass the best we could yesterday," she explained, setting her fork down. "But there are so many side trails we didn't have time to go down. And there are almost infinite options for places he could have taken her off a trail."

"He? So you're sure enough she was taken?"

Her shoulders fell. "It's what I'm most afraid of in the world."

"But?"

She shook her head and blinked, trying to hold back the tears she could feel stinging in her eyes. "It's likely. More likely than the idea that she just wandered off on her own."

"She was hiking alone, though?"

Bre nodded. "None of her friends have been reported missing, so the assumption is that she was alone."

"No friends you don't know about? No boys she could have met without you knowing it?"

"And then wandered out into the wilderness with?" She was shaking her head again. "I don't think so. And her car was parked near the entrance to the pass, so we know she was there and not lying to us about going hiking."

"Stranger things have happened."

"Not with Addy. She's a good kid. Besides, the chances of her innocently getting lost and then me being shot at are pretty slim, don't you think?"

He seemed to be considering it before resignation spread across his face too. "Okay, so she was likely taken. In that case, we're investigating a crime. The search angle changes then, as you might remember from last time we worked together."

She'd helped him search, but only in the capacity of a representative of the Wolf River Police Department.

Whether he liked it or not, she needed him. "If you're up for it, I can show you on the map where I'm thinking we should look."

"You brought a map with you?"

She grinned and shrugged, looking the slightest bit embarrassed, which only made her more adorable. "I hoped you'd say yes—"

"Stop." He cut her off, much like she'd done to him earlier. "I said yes, but I still think there are better options, better searchers." She heard the uncertainty in his voice. Even if they could never be more than friends, she wished she could help him see himself the way she saw him.

* * *

"Why can't you just accept my thanks and—"

Griffin shook his head. "Please. Just drop it. I'm helping—let's leave it there."

She stopped that time, but the way she looked at him said plenty. So she believed in him. That was fine. She shouldn't, because he wasn't anything special, but she did.

He felt her hand on his arm before he knew what was happening. She squeezed it lightly. "Thank you for helping."

Griffin nodded once. "So, where on this map were you planning to investigate?"

"I thought if we could follow this trail up further this way…" She pointed to where she meant, pausing halfway through. She jerked her gaze from the map, her eyes wide. "What was that?"

Griffin stilled and listened. A shiver shuddered through him, for reasons he couldn't articulate. He hadn't heard anything. But Bre had. He looked over at Ember. Her ears were pricked; she was listening.

"She hears it too," Bre said, her voice lower now.

Ember let out a low growl. Flapjack moved from his spot on the couch to the back door and growled too.

"The dogs' growling isn't making this less creepy." Her voice was only a whisper now, and she spoke in even tones, but Griffin heard the fear in Bre's voice.

Wait inside for a threat to come to them or go out and meet it? Typically he'd rather confront direct danger head-on than wait for it to creep up on him.

Bre seemed to agree because she was moving toward the front door, evidently hoping to go outside and investigate without scaring away whatever was near the back door attracting the attention of the dogs. "Why didn't I have my weapon with me last night?" she whispered frustratedly. He had no good answers for her, since he'd wanted to ask her the same question.

He moved to the small safe in the corner of his living room and pulled out a handgun for himself and one for Bre, racking the slides to chamber a round in each.

"The safety is off."

"Thanks." She inspected the weapon and assumed an easy down-and-ready position with the gun pointing at the floor. "I'd rather not go out there completely unarmed."

"Same." Though something told Griffin that being armed didn't necessarily make them safe. They still had to pinpoint where the threat was. And if the churning anxiety in his gut was correct, the person already knew right where they were.

"Out this way?" She motioned to the front door.

"You're the cop," he reminded her. The flash of insecurity in her eyes told him he wasn't the only one who struggled with self-doubt. Why had he never seen that about Bre before? He always thought of her as so unbreakable that it was hard to reconcile that with what he knew to be true about her past. "But I think yes."

She nodded, eased the front door open.

"Ember, heel," he commanded her. "Flapjack, heel."

Flapjack talked back at him, a combination between a whine and a growl that he'd only ever heard huskies make. "I said what I said," he whispered to the dog. Flapjack said nothing, just looked up at him.

They crept out into cool morning air. It was too still,

that uncomfortable calm that always seems to mean something is just about to go wrong.

"I changed my mind, get inside," he whispered to Bre, but she was moving forward and didn't seem to hear him.

"Bre," he whispered louder, not willing to draw any extra attention to them, but suddenly extremely uncomfortable with the idea of being outside. *God is that You, warning me?* "We need to get inside now."

"I thought—"

The whoosh that followed made his breath catch in his throat. The arrow hit two feet to the left of Bre.

"Inside, now!" he yelled, not caring how bossy he sounded when her life was on the line. She scrambled toward him and the door, slipping on the gravel rocks as she did so. He reached out to grab her arm to steady her. *Woosh.* Only six inches away from her that time. He pulled her to him, wrapped an arm around her and ran for the door, almost throwing them both inside with so much force that they landed on the floor. He scrambled to get to his knees and reached back to shut the door.

Bre was sitting there where she'd fallen, blinking.

"You okay? Did you hit your head?"

She shook the aforementioned slowly. "No, I'm okay. But..." She blinked a few more times and cleared her throat. Then she went back to law enforcement mode, as he liked to think of it, when her face was serious and focused on the job at hand and she was able to analyze what had happened.

The problem was, Griffin couldn't decide if that was a good thing entirely. Didn't a person have to take a minute to breathe, think, feel?

Then again, who was he to judge someone for not

wanting to sit in and work through uncomfortable feelings? He'd run away so he hadn't had to work through his.

"We need to call this in." She was already pulling her cell phone out of her pocket, so he let her handle it and listened as she gave the dispatcher all the relevant details about their situation.

Finally, he stood, reaching out a hand to offer to help her up. She took it.

"Someone really doesn't want you to investigate," he commented.

Bre nodded. She was frowning, her eyes focused on some point across the room. "Which is strange, isn't it? The Echo Pass Hunter has never much cared before if we searched." Slowly, she brought her gaze up to meet his. "I think that means Addy is alive."

"How do you figure?"

She crossed the room then walked back. "Every time someone has been killed or gone missing in the pass, we have searched it, and nothing like this has happened. There have been no signs there was a threat."

"Did you search this long after every one?" Griffin knew of the Echo Pass Hunter. Due to the digital nature of his job, he couldn't ignore social media rumors, even though he might like to. While promoting his business and connecting with clients, he had noticed fear sweeping through the town at the idea of a serial killer in their beloved wilderness area. But he hadn't followed the story as closely as some, didn't always read the news in the paper, and wasn't sure if he had the whole picture or not.

"We did," Bre confirmed. "It's standard practice for us to search past the initial twenty-four hours, but the press tends to lose their minimal attention span after that point, and we also scale down operations when someone makes the call that it's likely—" her voice broke slightly "—a recovery operation rather than a rescue."

"But you're still hoping for a rescue in this case."

Something in the way she looked at him after his statement shook him to the core. Her clear green eyes were unguarded, and he caught a brief flicker of pain.

Taking her in his arms now would be entirely inappropriate.

"I think you'll get it," he said, hoping the words would embrace her when he couldn't.

Her expression seemed to soften, the edges of it tinged with hope. "I want that to be true," she said, meeting his eyes then turning and pacing across the room again. "But I can't sit here and keep being a target. If he's willing to come after me like this, I think it means she's alive. What if he doesn't have her? What if she did get lost hiking in the pass and he heard about it and now he's tracking her?"

Griffin moved to the kitchen and pulled a notebook and a pencil out of the drawer, jotting down what she'd just asked.

"Or maybe he attempted to abduct her and she got away?"

He wrote that down, too, though it seemed unlikely. But as soon as he'd mentally dismissed the thought, he remembered that the Bible said "Nothing is impossible with God." He didn't know chapter and verse, but it was there somewhere.

Did he believe it?

All these years, he felt like he'd been able to run.

From people, guilt, even God, to a degree. Sure, he'd stayed on good terms with God overall, told himself that relationship was fine even if the others were ashes, but wasn't Griffin holding God at arm's length like he did everyone else? He hadn't gone to church since Megan's death, but he read his Bible daily. Prayed. Still believed. But hadn't he scaled down his expectations of God to make sure he couldn't be disappointed? Closeness, to a person, to the God who created the world, made you vulnerable.

Griffin was tired of being vulnerable.

He looked up at Bre. She likely understood that better than anyone, yet she was willing to put her heart out there. Look how she cared about Addy. She'd been hurt but it hadn't broken her.

"What if he's got her somewhere, and she's alive, but he doesn't want you to find her?"

"Why would he deviate from his MO though? If he's already taken her..." Bre shook her head. "I want to hope, too, more than anyone, but he kills women, Griffin. He doesn't abduct them."

"Does he? Or does he abduct them and kill them later?"

Her expression shifted. "I hope for their sakes he kills them immediately."

Serial murderers weren't known for their kindness to victims if they interacted with them before they died. Griffin hoped that idea was wrong, but wrote it down too.

"We need to get to the pass. Today. Could we take Ember and go?"

"We'll do better than that. We'll take all four."

She grinned and reached for him, pulling him to her

in a hug. His heartbeat quickened at the closeness and then, just as quickly, she let him go. "Let's pack what we need and go. Thanks for helping. I have a really good feeling about you and your dogs searching."

Her good feelings were the perfect counterpoint to his feelings. He had the awful certainty that the deeper they got into this case, the more they'd find they were learning things they wished they hadn't known.

That was, if they even had time to investigate. Griffin was still concerned that they wouldn't get the chance. Someone clearly wanted Bre dead. He was going to do everything in his power not to let that happen. He could do the work he needed to do for his online dog training at night. Daytime would be devoted to this case as far as he was concerned.

He could sleep when this was over.

Griffin didn't know if Bre would be able to join him on all the searches or if she still had to work. Either way, he was committed to seeing this through. He looked over at Ember, who caught his gaze and jumped down from the chair she'd been resting on.

"Help me not let her down, okay, girl?" he whispered.

She stretched her nose to the sky as he petted behind her ears and under her chin, but her eyes looked worried.

Too much was riding on this case. All of them—Griffin, Bre, Ember and Addy, most of all—needed his negative feelings to be wrong.

SIX

Having a target on her back was an uncomfortable way to live, Bre decided. After she'd called in the arrows, officers had been sent to the scene to investigate. Griffin hadn't been happy with the idea of her going back outside until backup arrived, and while she'd wanted to fight him on it, she'd suspected he was being wise and hadn't argued.

"I'm not done investigating, though, you know that, right?" She looked over at him as the last squad car pulled out of his driveway.

"So you mentioned," he said almost lazily, his voice not betraying stress or any other kind of emotion. Bre admired him for that; her own emotions had been wildly unpredictable the last few days. She wished she could have that calm for a minute, even if it was manufactured.

"So we'll load up the dogs?"

Griffin whistled and the two SAR huskies came running toward him. Ember's reddish fur gleaming even brighter in the sun. It was easy to see how she'd gotten her name. Flapjack, the easygoing husky, looked more like a yellow lab to Bre.

"And they're both huskies?" She raised her eyebrows. "Because I don't know how to tell you this, but they don't like that alike."

"Alaskan huskies. It's not technically an official breed, but surely you've heard of Alaskan Huskies or 'Alaskans' as some people up here call them, before."

"They're what people use in the Iditarod, right?"

Griffin nodded.

The dogs hovered at his ankles, weaving around each other and looking up at him intermittently, like they were waiting for instructions.

"They're both trained as search dogs?"

"Yes."

"Well, let's head to the pass then. I'll meet you up there?"

"We can ride together."

"What was the point of having my car towed if you're not going to let me use it?" she asked. Of course, the word *let* wasn't entirely accurate as it wasn't within his power to *let* her do anything. But she still found it funny that he would go to the trouble of making sure she had her own vehicle and then say they should ride together.

"Did you forget last night already? We'll ride together."

She shivered at the reminder and nodded.

"I didn't mean..." he started as they climbed into his truck, following the four dogs who had leapt into the backseat at his command second before.

"I know."

"Do you?" He looked over at her, pausing. He'd shut his door and buckled his seat belt, but he hadn't started the engine yet, his right hand still hovering near the ignition switch.

And Bre found that she couldn't look away. "You didn't mean to hurt me just now."

"By bringing up last night. But I did, didn't I?"

She shrugged and managed to tear her gaze from his. She focused out the window instead. "No one likes to be reminded of their mistakes, I guess."

"You think last night was a mistake."

"I was careless. I should have let you know I was coming, should have had a gun. I'm not thinking clearly. I want Addy back and I want that right now."

"Sounds like you're not really trusting God."

Her head whipped up, but his expression betrayed nothing. So it hadn't been meant as a pointed remark? Had he ever even realized she didn't believe like he did? Had she realized?

"I don't trust Him at all," she admitted, watching his expression. His brows knit together. In confusion? Anger?

"But..."

"I don't see a reason to. It's fine if you do, I wouldn't want to stop anyone else from believing in what they want, but are you listening to yourself? You're commenting that I'm not trusting a God who, according to you, let my niece be kidnapped."

"Your niece believes though. I've seen her at church and she's given her testimony before."

"Testimony?" Bre asked. The term was a legal one to her, meant for courtrooms and witnesses. She'd never heard it in any kind of religious context. Her experience with church and religion had been brief. She'd believed as a child and had even prayed at a Vacation Bible School and asked Jesus to save her. She'd wholeheartedly believed that He'd died on the cross to pay for her sins, that He *loved* her.

And then life had happened. Her mom had been taken away. She and Ben had been abandoned again and again. That was when Bre decided all those stories must have just been…stories.

"She's told about what Jesus has done in her life. How He's helped her, things like that."

She nodded but said nothing. Now wasn't the time to get into a religious discussion with him, when they'd finally found some kind of level footing in their friendship, so she hoped they could just let it go.

"And Ben believed."

Clearly, Griffin hadn't picked up on her subtle hints. She knew her brother had hung onto the faith she'd been unable to keep. That didn't change how she felt about it all.

"Could we talk about this later, Griffin? Or not at all, but later if it's something you want to bring up again? I can't do this today." She could hear in his voice that this was something that was important to him, not something he did for anyone else, and she couldn't bear to disappoint him today.

"Sure, no problem. Let's talk about what we're going to do up at the pass. You mentioned wanting to go into some of the places you hadn't searched the other day. Did you bring the map?"

Her shoulders relaxed at the change in topic; this one was much easier for her to handle. Bre reached into her pocket and unfolded the map she'd brought.

"As much of this area as we can cover would be great. I'm not going to lie, Griffin, I'm at a loss right now. There's no strategy for me at the moment other than covering a large amount of area and trying to see if maybe Addy is there, or some kind of evidence exists to say that she was there and gives us a starting point for a search."

She finally hazarded a glance back at him. His attention was on the road. "How would you do it?"

"Hmm…" As he considered the question, he stayed focused on what he was doing, giving Bre a minute to study him. The years had aged him slightly, she decided, but only in the best of ways. His stubble was a little rougher, his jawline sharper. He looked like he'd fought something inside and felt like he'd lost; there was a hint of sadness around his eyes that hadn't been there before. "I haven't worked as many searches where a criminal was strongly believed to be involved, but it does change the process some."

"How?"

"In some ways, I guess it doesn't. We're trained to always assume it could be criminal activity and be looking for evidence police could use later. As you know, a lot of times, we work with law enforcement and they're the ones looking for that evidence. But it changes how we search because it makes lost people behave in different ways. Maybe they were being chased by a criminal. People have actually done studies to find out how different types of people behave when they're lost in the wilderness."

"And someone who was running from someone would behave differently from someone who was trying to get home."

"Right. Instinct might cause the running person to go deeper into the wilderness, for shelter. Whereas someone who is just lost might be trying to find open areas to find their way out of the woods."

"But," Bre said slowly, "it's possible we *and* the Echo Pass Hunter are both looking for her. She may have just gotten lost and now she's in danger. And she might not even know that. So should we factor that in instead?"

He looked at her, didn't say anything.

At first, she said nothing, just stared back, realizing that, without doing it on purpose, she'd raised her chin slightly. The longer he didn't say anything, the more she tried to ignore his implication until finally she blew out a breath.

"Fine. It's not probable. So let's approach it like there's criminal involvement."

"Better safe than sorry."

He parked the truck in the lot and Bre avoided the area where her niece's car had been parked. The chief had had the car towed to the police department, since it was possible there could be some kind of evidence in it. Bre wanted to have a look around in it herself, in case there was some clue that could shed light on where Addy was now. But even in the emotional state she found herself in now, she knew that having the evidence technicians and crime scene guys look over it first was the best idea. They were used to reading what objects said, seeing a story in a perfectly ordinary looking scene. Bre didn't know how they did it.

Still, it was her niece who was missing. So, on the off chance she might notice something as significant that they hadn't noticed, she planned to ask the chief if she could take a look at it.

Not today though. Today she was hoping inspecting the car wouldn't be necessary. That maybe, despite days of nothing, today would be the day they'd find some kind of lead and Addy herself.

Alive.

"Where should we start?" Griffin asked her, and she wished he'd just pick one of the locations she'd mentioned and take charge of the search.

Bre opened her mouth to say so when she caught his expression. Uncertain. He still wasn't sure he was the best man for this job, she realized with a start. He'd said as much earlier, but she'd written it off as run-of-the-mill insecurity that crept in to give everyone doubts now and then. She hadn't really thought he could possibly truly believe that.

He did though.

Besides, was she the cop here or not? It was time she started acting like one. Being hysterical wasn't going to find her niece.

She took a deep breath. "Let's head toward Sunrise Ridge."

"That's a fifteen-mile roundtrip."

"Too much for the dogs?"

He barely concealed a snort and, when she looked at him, his eyes were almost dancing. "They can do twice that without needing more than a quick break. It was just a comment."

"I don't think we'll make it all the way there. I want to explore the small trails that shoot off that main path though. We spent a little time there the other night, up to the avalanche spot."

"So, three miles in."

Bre nodded.

"Sounds like a plan. Lead on."

Bre climbed out of the truck, shut the door and started

for the pass, butterflies churning in her stomach. She was afraid of what they would find, or not find, afraid of who might find them.

After this morning, she couldn't pretend the arrows shot at her yesterday were just because she'd been in the pass and a woman who fit the serial killer's victim profile.

Whether she liked it or not, she had a target on her back now. She'd put one on Griffin's back, too, by asking him to get involved.

And the dogs?

She looked over at the K-9s weaving around Griffin's ankles as he loaded his backpack and then reached for their search harnesses. They were adorable. Flapjack was extremely sweet and seemed so in tune with people's emotions. And Ember seemed like she was smarter than half the people Bre knew. What if, because of her, something happened to them?

This wouldn't drag on, this search. Bre wouldn't let it. They were going to find Addy.

And they were all going to get out of this alive.

They'd stopped at Bre's house to get a pair of Addy's dirty socks for the dogs to scent, which Griffin had them sniff right after dressing them in their harnesses—officially cuing that it was a workday—and then gave the command to search. The dogs loved having a job, Griffin had found, and they needed cues to know what was being asked of them and to be able to do it. Some people trained their K-9s to alert to any living people within a given area, but Griffin's search was specifically for one person. He explained this to Bre as they started toward the trailhead and she nodded slowly, like she was trying to take it all in.

When they got to the marker that designated the start of the trail, Griffin looked over at Bre. "Left?"

She nodded. The trail crisscrossed the land, with multiple options stretching out in different directions. This trail, which led northeast, was the direction Bre had felt hadn't been searched enough, so they were going to try to rule it out.

"What if we don't find anything?" she asked, her voice uncertain.

"Then we will still have found *something*. We will have at least found a spot where she isn't, and narrowed it down that way."

"That's true." She breathed out, her shoulders sagging a little. "I want to find something."

"Me too." Griffin nodded up to his K-9s, who were searching, noses in the air, catching currents of smell that humans rarely thought about but that dogs noticed. "So do they."

The first few miles of the trail passed easily, up to the point of the avalanche. A group of Wolf River police officers was up there, and there was a black body bag on the snow.

Bre's eyes widened and he thought her face paled as well.

"It's probably Megan," he reminded her, but she didn't look like she was reassured.

"I'll go talk to them to double check."

It gave Griffin time to give the dogs a drink of water and a minute to rest. When Bre walked back to them, she looked a little better, though still a little desperate.

"You were right."

"I'm glad they're finally taking her out of the mountains. Her family needed the closure."

"And you, too, I would imagine." Her voice was light enough, not demanding a story he didn't want to tell, which he appreciated. That gave Griffin the space to feel like it was his decision whether to share or not, and he wanted to, at least right now, with Bre.

"You knew we dated once."

She nodded, but her expression gave nothing away. It wasn't that he wanted her to be jealous, but he did wonder whether she cared. He couldn't help it.

"We were friends after. Actually, we were friends the whole time and it was just kind of clear we were both better off that way," he continued. He glanced over at Bre now and then, but also up ahead at the dogs who were staying within sight but running left and right around the trails. He appreciated their canvassing a bit extra. Covering more ground was another benefit to using dogs for a search. But Griffin never made a habit of assuming an area was clear just because his K-9s had been there. Just like people, they could make mistakes or miss something. But usually he was the one who made the mistake. He had learned to follow one of the most important rules of search-and-rescue work, which was to trust your dog.

"That doesn't mean you don't need closure. Friends matter too."

There seemed to be more to her words than a discussion of him and Megan, so Griffin chose his words carefully.

"They do. Friends are important. Extremely so." He didn't look away from Bre as he spoke, but she broke his stare and turned away. Her unspoken message was received. He'd abandoned his friends when he'd retreated from the world.

They'd reached the top of a ridge. "Where to from here? Over and down that slope? Or along the ridge-line?"

Bre seemed to be considering their options and, as she thought, the dogs ran up and down the ridgeline. Flapjack caught Griffin's attention. He seemed focused on something in the air, but hadn't alerted yet. He was a great dog with potential, but he was young and didn't always have the confidence he needed yet.

Ember's ears were moving back and forth, too, though. Finally, she ran to Griffin, barked, and ran back to the spot where she'd been, looking down over a slope that Griffin could see was heavily treed at the bottom.

"Good girl. You smell her, don't you?"

Ember lifted her head, her eyes bright and ears perked, seemed pleased her hard work was being recognized.

"Let's search down this way." Griffin motioned toward the trees. It was common for people to go down a mountain to try to find safety; he had learned that in many of the classes he'd taken. Maybe there would be a creek somewhere in those trees; if Addy was alive, maybe she had gone that way to get access to water. One of the biggest dangers in the woods wasn't wildlife or exposure, but old-fashioned dehydration. People only had three days without water before their bodies shut down and died, and Griffin had seen too many who hadn't made it because of a lack of access to this resource.

Hopefully, Addy, raised in Alaska by a dad who'd loved the outdoors, would know that finding water had to be a priority.

If she'd been moving through the wilderness of her own free will, which Griffin wasn't sure of anymore.

"Why would she have hiked this far alone?" Bre asked as they slowly descended the mountainside. The trail here wasn't very well trodden, just a narrow, weathered switchback that appeared to drop straight down again once it made its way partway along the mountain.

"Maybe she didn't mean to. What are her hobbies?" Truth be told, Griffin thought it likely by now that Addy hadn't made it, that asking what her hobbies *were* might have been a more apt way to phrase the question. He'd also made it clear to his dogs that they were searching for Addy's scent and for a body, as well, though he obviously hoped it was the first. But someone had to be realistic in this investigation and it wasn't going to be Bre.

They had made short work of the steepest part of the descent, and Griffin couldn't help but admire Bre. He'd never been able to find many good hiking partners who matched his pace, but she matched it—and him—well in so many ways.

"She likes to paint," Bre said, considering. "Sometimes she goes hiking with her camera and takes photos of scenery to recreate later."

"So she could have seen something—a moose, a bear—and followed it further than she'd meant to be... anything like that is an option."

"Maybe."

Bre might be being more realistic than Griffin had realized because her voice didn't carry the undiluted hope and determination he'd heard yesterday. It was if being out here and seeing the vastness of the land had somehow made her realize that Addy didn't have much of a chance.

Apart from God, Griffin realized almost immediately. God was capable of bigger things than they could imagine and, if it wasn't Addy's time to die, God could have kept her alive through the most harrowing of circumstances.

That was the hope he had to cling to. He wished Bre did too. He wasn't under the impression that faith was important to her, though he wasn't sure they'd ever talked about it.

"There's still a chance, Bre," he said aloud to her. "Even if…"

"Even if she's gone, your God is still good, right?"

Her voice was hard; so bitter that it took Griffin off guard and he had to blink. Her tone and words left little doubt that she did not believe like he did.

"I was going to say even if the murderer is after her, he's not stronger than God. She's still got a chance."

She stopped so suddenly that Griffin almost ran into her as she spun around to face him. She barely came up to his chest, on level ground anyway, and now they were hiking downhill and she was ahead.

"Don't talk to me about a God who would let a child get lost like this. Ever. Again."

A wave of nausea washed over him and he realized just how much Bre *didn't* believe. Had he been fooling himself to think she wasn't as far away from God as she'd indicated in earlier conversations? Probably. That could happen when you wanted something so much. And in this case Griffin had wanted her to have a relationship with God for so many reasons. Most importantly, because it was her only hope for peace, now and in eternity. God made it clear that Jesus was the only way to Heaven, through His work on the cross. If Bre had rejected that… The alternative was awful to think about. Eternal separation from a God who Griffin was confident loved them.

But had anyone ever turned to Jesus because someone argued them into it? Griffin doubted it. Instead he took a deep breath of cool mountain air and prayed to the God who had made these mountains, both for Bre's heart and that she would see a miracle. In this case, that she would find her niece alive and see that if that happened, God was the only reason why.

SEVEN

There was no reason not to be losing hope. Bre's chest was tight and her mind was racing. She was trying so hard, and it wasn't enough; it was never going to be enough to find Addy.

Setting out with the dogs had buoyed her hopes a little, but then they'd gotten out here and the landscape was just so big. Too big for a teenager to be out in alone. Bre hated to think of it, but she knew what had probably happened to Addy.

Bre missed her brother. She missed Addy.

Griffin was right here with her, but she missed him too. Why did everyone she cared about leave?

She took a deep breath and exhaled, though it did nothing to soothe her. Since her emotions didn't appear to be listening to any polite requests to calm down and stop panicking, she decided to try to distract herself instead. So Bre watched Ember. As someone who wasn't a dog handler, she didn't know quite what she was looking for, though Bre thought she might if she saw it. Griffin was keeping a close eye on both dogs, too, and he knew what they were saying with their behavior and body language. It impressed her how they could work as a team. Just another part of what made him so attractive.

He hadn't said anything else after she'd shut down yet another attempt at religious conversation on his behalf. Bre couldn't decide if she'd offended him or if he was just respecting her wishes and letting that line of thinking go. It was too much for her handle after everything she'd seen, not just with Addy, but her own childhood. Her line of work. All of it. Nothing about a good God made sense to her after what she'd witnessed, and life was supposed to make *sense*. Wasn't it?

"Why did she get a scent earlier and now she just seems to be walking again? Does she still have it or…" Bre finally broke the silence because she needed to know. Knowing what was going on seemed worth the risk of talking to Griffin again.

A glance at him showed his demeanor to still be fairly easy and relaxed. His shoulders weren't tense and nothing in his body language that she could see seemed to indicate that he was uncomfortable with her now, or anything like that. Was it possible for a man to be that patient?

His response to her earlier bitterness about God didn't make sense to her. Could anyone really care that deeply about everything he said and did, have that much courage of conviction? And then still be kind when she didn't agree with him? Yet another thing that puzzled her about this man.

"I don't think she has the scent anymore." He slowed his steps then shook his head and spoke again. "Actually, honestly, I'm *sure* she doesn't."

"So why are we still going this way?"

"Because she had it earlier. That means this is still

worth investigating. Air currents do strange things to scents. The time of day, the weather, all of that affects the way the scent particles disperse in the air. It's still morning, so scent is more likely to carry upward, which means we can't rule out this area. The smell could have carried. Have a little hope, will you?"

That word again. She should have been thankful he wasn't already mad at her, but her emotions were on edge right now and Bre almost told him exactly what she thought of that word. To her, it meant nothing good since it always seemed to be used to describe *false* hope, at least in her experience. Her mom had *hoped* rehab would help her overcome her drug addiction. Doctors had *hoped* Ben would survive after his car wreck. Hope, as far as Bre was concerned, was nothing more than a well-intentioned lie. She didn't get a chance to tell him her thoughts on the word, though, because Ember started to bark. Bre looked back at the dog, who was running up ahead, barking, and then running back to Griffin.

"Yes. Good girl."

Flapjack joined in after another couple of seconds with his nose in the air and Griffin praised him too.

They hurried to catch up to the dogs where they'd settled in a thick stand of alders. Bre shivered, her natural fear of bears creeping in, but the animals didn't seem uncomfortable, just excited. She guessed she should trust that if something dangerous was around, they'd let them know somehow. If that was something a dog could do.

"Ember alerted even more strongly here than earlier. This is good." Griffin grabbed Bre's upper arm as he hurried past her. "See?" He grinned and it was the biggest smile seen from him in years.

Maybe she'd consider a tiny bit of hope. Just a sliver.

There was nothing remarkable about where the K-9s were sitting—not that Bre could see. Certainly no sign of Addy herself.

"But they're sure she was here?" she asked Griffin, not quite remembering how the process worked. While she'd had a brief class on search dogs at the police academy, it had been very general. Most law enforcement officers she knew had to rely on trained SAR workers to help them know how the dogs played into the search and what they were capable of. She'd worked with Griffin on a couple of searches before and knew he'd explained some of this, but her memory and skills were rusty.

"Without a doubt. There's a good scent pool here, from their reaction, so I'd say she might have rested here."

"Or…" She swallowed hard. "She could have been… could have died…"

Griffin shook his head.

"They don't detect that?"

"They do," he said slowly. "But this isn't how they'd alert to it. Addy was alive when she was here."

Chills ran down her arms and Bre found herself immediately blinking as tears stung in her eyes. She had been *alive*: right here!

"Recently?"

"I can't tell you that. Neither can they. But she was alive here. Be happy for that."

Griffin was on his hands and knees, searching the area. Bre dropped down beside him.

"No sign of blood. Not that I can see, and typically

this isn't how they'd act for blood. Wait…" He reached into the brush and pulled out a tiny piece of fabric, purple and shiny.

"Addy's jacket." Bre knew it immediately, her breath catching in her throat. Her muscles tensed in anticipation. Finally, *finally* they had something to work with.

"More proof she was here, in case you doubted the dogs."

She hadn't, but more proof always made her feel better. You couldn't have too much certainty in Bre's world.

"We're going to find her, Bre. I really think we're going to find her."

But would they find her before the Echo Pass Hunter did? Or before he found them?

As if in some kind of answer, a cloud moved over the sun at that exact moment, dimming the light in the area and causing the temperature to drop several degrees. Bre shivered. One step forward, but would it be enough?

How much could she afford to get her hopes up? Maybe not much at all.

And one thing was even more certain. They were still in danger, maybe more so, and they couldn't afford to let down their guard.

She felt the same way she had yesterday, right before the arrows had started flying when she and the chief had found Megan's body.

Ember suddenly let out a low growl.

"Griffin…" Bre trailed off. He was fully focused on his dog. Flapjack's body position wasn't reassuring either. His head was down, his fur raised on his back, and he'd positioned himself in front of Bre.

They stood, frozen, for at least five minutes. Then both dogs relaxed.

"We have to get out of here," Griffin finally said.

"But we just found…" She wanted to argue, but his eyes were full of fear.

"I think we have been found too. Or are close to being found. Something is out there, Bre. Or someone. The search is no longer safe today. Risk levels just got too high."

They couldn't just stop searching. They had to keep going…

But Griffin's dogs seemed to agree and were already heading back up the hill, on a slightly different path than they'd taken down.

A thought struck her. What if they were being followed by the Echo Pass Hunter right now? What if this time he didn't shoot at her but just waited… What if they led the killer straight to Addy?

"We'll come back, sweetie," She whispered into the air, hoping somehow if Addy was alive, she would know that Bre wasn't giving up. "Please be okay."

They started back for the trailhead. The hair on the back of Bre's neck stayed up all the way until they'd dropped back down on the other side of the ridgeline, where the dogs had first alerted.

They'd made progress today. She had to hold on to that, but fear still clawed at her. They were getting closer.

But so was the killer.

After a full day, Bre came home to a house that was just as messy as she'd left it the night she was run off the road. Last night? Had it been that recently? She felt like it had been weeks since then.

Sleep was what she really needed, but the dishes in

the sink would smell if she didn't take care of them, and Bre hated messes, especially in the kitchen. The kitchen where she'd spent her formative years must have had counters, but Bre had never seen them. They had been too full of used paper plates, stacked and piled on top of rotting bananas, bills and empty beer bottles. Bre didn't drink, so keeping her space clear of alcohol containers was easy. And she had a general dislike of papers plates, probably due to the fact that was all she could remember eating off of as a kid. They weren't always clean paper plates either; sometimes they'd have to be reused. She'd vowed long ago never to let her kitchen look like that one had, with its air of neglect and despair. Order wasn't an option for her, not if she wanted to feel comfortable in her own house. Bre knew it was a control issue, a trauma response, but it was one that worked for her.

So she made sure her gun was in her holster at her waistband, just in case, got herself a glass of ice water and took a long drink, still feeling the effects of hiking all day after being awake for half the night. Her mind felt foggy and her muscles ached. She had the beginnings of a headache pounding on one side of her head. It was worth it, though, for what they'd found. She knew now what Addy had been wearing, something she had called the chief about on her way home to let him know. He added it to the description they'd sent out. It wasn't much, but it could still help.

And more importantly, it told them where Addy had been. They had a lead now, somewhere to search, and that was one of the best things Bre could have hoped for today.

She finished the dishes and shut the water off. The

silence in the house hummed in her ears. It was over-whelming after the noise of the day. People thought of the outdoors as quiet and, while it was peaceful, it wasn't at all. Especially not with two dogs. They were more well behaved than any she'd ever been around, but they still barked on occasion at a ground squirrel, or at the wind, or at any number of things.

Possibly at the Echo Pass Hunter?

She knew the dogs hadn't found Addy herself. But they'd smelled something, more than once, and had be-haved in a way that made Griffin uncomfortable. She'd seen it in his reaction.

A shiver ran down her spine, the silence of the house and memories of the day too much for her to take at one time without being uncomfortable.

How close had they been to a killer today? There was no way of knowing, but Bre was sure it was closer than she was comfortable with. Most of the crimes they worked in Wolf River involved property. There was the occasional violent offense, but she'd worked very few murders and no prior ones involving serial killers. The idea that a person could be this evil overwhelmed her with a sense of oppressing darkness. Any sense of elation she'd felt when they'd discovered evidence that Addy might have been alive and moving through the pass of her own free will had disappeared when she'd become conscious of the closeness of the threat.

There was no reason for the killer to follow them be-sides wanting to know where Addy was. That meant he might not have her.

But that didn't mean Addy was safe. Or Bre. Maybe not Griffin either.

Much as Bre needed it, sleep wasn't happening, not

anytime soon. Instead Bre spent time wandering around the house, tidying things that didn't need tidying, and finding things to clean. She'd just finished the baseboards when she heard a noise outside, like a soft footstep, outside.

Her body responded before her mind even had a chance, her palms breaking into a sweat and her heart immediately pounding in her chest. She had to stay calm. But Bre was finding there was a massive difference between investigating a situation that she didn't have a personal connection to and being the possible target of a killer. Her training still came to mind, just not as fast, and she had to fight through anxiety to get back to it.

First, she moved to her bedroom, got her sidearm out of her safe, grabbed a holster from the shelf where she kept them, and secured her weapon at her hip. Then she moved back down the stairs, listening.

The noise had come from outside, she was pretty sure. It crossed her mind to text Griffin, but he was too far away. Besides, she didn't want to be bothering him all the time. He'd given in and agreed to help her search, and every minute of today had shown Bre that she might have gotten him deeper involved in something than she'd meant to. She almost called the chief, but she couldn't be sure she'd even heard anything outside. Appearing paranoid might cost her her spot working on this case. She needed to act like the law enforcement professional she was, not a woman who was so on edge she panicked at every noise in the night. Instead, Bre started toward the backdoor, steps slow and careful.

Nothing. No more noises. Heartbeat whooshing in her ears, Bre reached for the doorknob and eased the back door open, immediately returning her right hand to her side, resting it on top of the holster. She could draw quick enough from here if it was necessary.

If she saw the threat before he managed to strike. It was safe to assume anyone who wanted to do her harm could be the Echo Pass Hunter.

His weapon of choice was a bow. All of the murders so far had been committed with a takedown bow, one that could easily come apart to be stored in a small space, that the killer likely hid in a hiking backpack and could easily assemble in the backcountry and still hit his target.

But if he was waiting in her backyard, could she be facing another kind of weapon? A knife?

From what they'd worked up at the police department as far as a profile, it was possible, even likely, that he could overpower her, even without a weapon, due to sheer size advantage. Their killer was likely a man, and she was a fairly petite woman. Their psychological profile saw him as a risk taker who didn't view his risks as dangerous. Ambushing her at her home would fit.

The night air was quiet and still, even though the sun was still up and the warm glow on the trees made it look earlier than it was: eleven o'clock.

Bre stood there on the back deck and waited. Half of her wanted to have imagined the noise and half of her wished she could somehow provoke the killer to step out of the shadows so she could face him once and for all And find out what had happened to Addy. She knew better than to think she'd ever get an answer to the question of *why* Addy was being targeted or had already been. Serial killers had patterns, but they left many questions unanswered, and Bre had stopped feeling frustrated at that. The day she fully understood the motives of a madman would be a concerning day indeed, so she was prepared to accept some unknowns.

But she couldn't handle this way of living much longer, looking over her shoulder, agonizing over whether Addy was okay, dodging arrows...

She needed this to end soon.

Keeping herself within sight of the back door, she scanned the yard for any sign of a threat. All seemed clear. Safe.

If only she felt safe or could imagine feeling safe anytime soon.

Bre went back inside, locked the door behind her and exhaled the breath she hadn't realized she'd been holding. The later it got, the jumpier she was getting. She'd probably heard a normal noise and overreacted, something that was more likely to keep happening as nighttime descended. She needed the rest if she was going to go out and search for Addy again tomorrow, which she was hoping to do, if Griffin said they could take the dogs out again.

Upstairs felt too far away, though, and not centrally located enough in her house to keep watch. The couch would suit her purposes tonight, giving her a place to at least catch some sleep between waking up at every noise, as she expected she would.

Still uneasy from earlier but trying to ignore it, Bre brushed her teeth, changed into sweatpants and a hoodie, and lay down on the couch, pulling a blanket over herself.

EIGHT

When she opened her eyes, it was dark. She hadn't heard anything but something kept her still, afraid to make a move lest someone hear her.

A soft thud from her laundry room confirmed what had woken her. Someone was inside her house. This time, she knew what she heard was a legitimate threat.

Slowly, she reached her left arm down to the floor, where she'd slid her service pistol underneath the couch when she'd laid down to sleep. She hadn't wanted it too far out of reach, in case anything happened.

Another noise. This one sounded like a footstep.

Too late to call for backup. Griffin, the police, no one could get here fast enough to help Bre, even if she was able to pull out her phone and send a message.

This was the meeting she'd almost hoped for earlier, but this wasn't the kind of confrontation she'd pictured. Bre wasn't in control, couldn't even see since the light outside had finally dimmed to twilight, leaving the inside of her house nothing but dark shadows layered on top of each other. Turning on a light would allow her to see, but if she was right that there was someone else in the house, it would allow them to see also. This was her territory; she had a slight advantage in the dark, and she would not give that up.

Bre had wanted answers, and an end to this, but it looked like, instead, the ending wouldn't be what she'd expected. She was at a disadvantage, vulnerable in the darkness, not knowing when her attacker would strike.

Something had to change.

Taking another deep breath, she pushed the blanket off herself, sat up and put her feet on the floor. Her best chance of surviving this confrontation was to make it one, not to sit on the couch waiting for him to come for her.

"Get out of my house!" she yelled.

A startled crash from the laundry room then silence. She thought she could hear slow footsteps in that direction, coming toward her. Stalking his prey.

Her training dictated that she should never shoot when she didn't know for sure what her target was, and Bre had no desire to kill an innocent person, or any purpose at all, so she held her fire but kept her hands on the weapon, at a down-and-ready position. Shadows moved to her right, in the direction the noise had come from.

Any confirmation that her life was in danger, and she could shoot. But she had to wait…

The now-familiar sound of an arrow flying echoed in the air, drowned out by the twang of the bowstring she'd never been close enough to hear before. The sound was a twanging thud, a threat in and of itself, and though it didn't hit her, Bre knew she was justified to shoot.

She fired in his direction, thankful the houses in her neighborhood were situated far apart. The caliber she was using couldn't penetrate through the outside of the house anyway, but the last thing she wanted was for a neighbor to hear and come investigate, maybe become collateral damage.

Another crash and a yell. She didn't think she'd hit him, but Bre was also fairly certain that the killer hadn't expected someone to shoot back at him.

Typically, his victims appeared to put up a fight, based on the bodies' examinations, but not until it was too late. Almost like their captor was someone they trusted, though it didn't seem to be possible that every woman who'd been killed in the past had known the same man, been connected to the same individual. The Wolf River Police Department had looked into it and had done extensive tracing of their contacts to try to find a connection, but there wasn't one between all of them.

Instead, it was likely a *type* of person they'd all been inclined to trust, or not notice, until it was too late. Some of the postmortems had indicated that the women had died after the initial shot with an arrow; sometimes they bore bruises or other signs of a struggle that indicated their deaths hadn't been immediately.

Briefly, Bre wondered what the FBI profilers would say about the killer's behavior tonight, and whether they would have expected it. If one of those agents was with her now, maybe she could predict his next move, but as it was, she was on her own.

The footsteps seemed to be retreating. Bre kept the gun up and started to relax. But then came a whoosh and a glancing pain in her upper arm.

He'd shot her.

She lifted her weapon and aimed. Fired again.

Another sound and her front door creaked open and slammed shut. She waited in the dark, not moving, in case it was a trick. But she heard noises outside that seemed to indicate he really was running away.

She'd won? At least this little battle?

Bre took a deep breath then another, trying to process what had just happened. She put a hand to her arm, and it pulled away, wet with what she presumed to be blood. She yanked her cell phone out of her back pocket.

"Nine-one-one. What's your emergency?"

"I've been shot," Bre told the dispatcher. "It's an arrow, and I think it's a graze more than anything, but I'd feel better if someone checked it out. It's not safe for me to leave the house. Don't send EMTs without an officer though. I believe I was attacked by a serial killer."

It was a testimony to the sort of special person it took to work dispatch that the calm voice on the other end of the line didn't even seem to hesitate. "All right, if you'll give me your address, we will have someone over there within five to seven minutes. Normally I would stay on the line, but we are short staffed tonight. Call again if anything changes. Otherwise they will be there within five to seven minutes."

A good response time, even for a small town like Wolf River, but Bre knew it would feel achingly long.

She wanted to call the chief. He'd always been there for her, but getting in touch with him when help was already on the way would look weak. She needed to handle this herself. She could wait.

A minute passed. Bre debated with herself for a second before she texted, but emotion won out over reason. She might not feel comfortable showing the chief how scared she was, but she could trust Griffin with this. She shouldn't be bothering Griffin, especially not when it felt like she was being a damsel in distress, but it wasn't as though she'd wanted to be attacked. Besides, he'd be hurt if he found out about it from anyone but her.

With that in mind, she tapped out a message.

Someone was in my house. Got shot with an arrow, but it's just a scrape. I'll let you know what the EMTs say. Still up for searching the pass again tomorrow?

Her message was meant to sound lighthearted. In truth, Bre felt anything but. They'd made so much progress today, yet here she was in danger again. How many close calls until someone got hurt?

And what about Addy? Was she hurt already?

Bre squeezed her eyes shut and sighed then opened them and sat on the couch, waiting for help to arrive.

Griffin hadn't made it all the way through the text before grabbing his gear and heading to his truck, followed closely by Ember and Flapjack.

Did she really think she could send a message like that and not have him show up? She sounded like she was okay, but the only person he knew with a bigger streak of hardheaded independence than Bre was…well, him. So he understood what it was like to face everything alone and maybe he just didn't want Bre to have to do that anymore.

He justified his hurrying to her house to himself all the way into town as he fought to keep his attention on the road. Bre was alive. He would know more details later, but for now that was what mattered, and the fact that she wasn't going to be alone for long.

In fact, he had every intention of letting one of the dogs stay with her. She didn't need to be alone in that house after this. It was good she'd become aware of the intruder tonight, but that didn't meant she would be aware next time. He'd rather her have an on-duty officer standing outside her house but that wasn't up to him.

Please don't let there be a next time, he prayed, doing his best to keep his foot light on the gas pedal and not break any traffic laws getting to her house.

He knew she was hurt—Bre had said as much in her message—but the sight of the ambulance in her driveway, with lights flashing, still made his breath catch. He wasted no time climbing out of the truck. He told the dogs to stay for now, hurrying through the open front door, frustration building within him.

A killer had taken a shot at her, several shots really, but had succeeded partially tonight, and someone had left her front door open?

His chest got tighter. Surely, nothing had happened in the time it had taken him to get there? If he was too late…

Imagination creating all kinds of worst-case scenarios, he hurried into her house, shutting the door behind himself and locking it.

Griffin rounded the corner to her living room and she was there, sitting on the couch, with an EMT leaning over her, bandaging her arm, and Griffin took a full breath for the first time since she'd texted him.

"You're okay?" he asked as he approached.

"Griffin, what are you doing here?"

"You're hurt."

"I didn't mean you had to come."

"I didn't feel like I had to."

He stood next to her, leaving plenty of room for the paramedic to work on her other side.

"How is she doing?" he asked the EMT whose name-tag said Waters. The medic looked at Bre, as though asking permission.

"It's fine if he knows," she said.

"She lost some blood, but not too much. It was mostly a graze— a bit of a nasty one. So it's minor, but definitely nothing to ignore. There's a risk of infection if she doesn't take care of it properly, and she needs to be mindful of it."

Griffin thought there was a pretty good chance Waters the EMT would say she didn't need to be hiking around a mountain pass in search of a serial killer, but was equally sure that Bre wouldn't care whether that was advisable or not. Personally, Griffin was still tense at the sight of her injured, though deeply relieved she was okay.

"I'll be right back," Griffin told Bre. He moved through the house, looking for any evidence the would-be killer had left behind. He was careful not to touch anything, since he knew the police would be coming to process the scene at some point. But he saw no evidence that the house was currently unsafe. Everything was locked tight. Of course, it had been before too.

Waters finished wrapping the wound and then started to pack up, nodding to his partner over in the corner. "We'll go ahead and head out now. I don't think there's any need for you to come into the hospital."

"Thanks." Bre sounded relieved.

An officer walked into the room then, not one that Griffin recognized, but Bre seemed to know him.

"We need to process the scene, but I called the Chief and he talked to the crime scene guys and they can't get out here to process it until morning."

"Small towns." Bre shook her head. "That's okay. I'll be here."

"Stay safe, okay? I'll drive past a couple extra times tonight."

And he followed the EMTs out.

Not wanting to risk the door being left open again, he walked them to the door and let them out, then went back to Bre.

"You really didn't have to come," she said again.

"When are you going to get it? I don't feel like I have to be there for you. I *want* to be there for you." He said it without weighting the consequences, and while it wasn't the confession of attraction she'd shut him down on earlier, he still worried it was too much and wondered if he should be more careful. She seemed to consider his words, though, and must have decided to appreciate them because she nodded and smiled.

"Thanks. You're always there when I need you, aren't you?"

"Not always. I missed a lot. I should have been there after Ben…"

"Let's not talk about that tonight."

He must have hurt her more than he'd realized, the way she avoided talking about it. He could spot self-protection a mile away; it was something he did often enough himself.

"All right, what should we talk about?"

She looked at him, eyebrow raised, surprise in her features. "You're staying?"

"Just for a little while. I didn't figure you'd want to be alone yet." He hesitated. Maybe he was reading the situation wrong and the last thing he wanted to do was to be in her way when she wanted to be alone.

"I don't."

He settled on the couch then stood. "Mind if I get the dogs out of the truck? I left them out there when I came in."

"Sure. You know I love your dogs."

It took less than a minute to release the K-9s from the truck and get back to Bre's side, which was good because he wasn't comfortable leaving her right now. He couldn't stay here the rest of the night, even with a really good reason, because there were people who would read into it and make assumptions. Griffin wasn't willing to do anything that would damage Bre's reputation.

Both dogs immediately jumped up beside Bre on the couch, Flapjack more on her lap than beside her, so Griffin took a chair.

She was smiling, and he felt his shoulders relax. This was proving to be one of the most difficult tests of faith he'd ever been through. It was one thing to trust God for his own safety, but to have to trust him for someone he cared about more than he cared about himself? This was new to Griffin.

But as much as it…well, he should just admit it. It scared him. As much as it scared him, he'd rather be here with Bre and scared than anywhere else without her and not scared.

He'd spent years telling himself they'd never have made it as more than friends. He was starting to wonder if he'd wasted years lying to himself. And if there was any hope in the future of trying again.

Bre wouldn't have said that the events of the night or even the long day that had preceded it disappeared entirely in Griffin's presence, but the fact that his presence did *something* to her wasn't something she could deny anymore.

When he'd first brought the dogs in, they'd practically attacked her with kisses and she'd had to laugh at their enthusiasm. He'd told them to stay on the couch so they didn't contaminate the scene, which she appreciated. She'd thought Griffin would leave any minute; she knew his faith was important to him and people he went to church with might judge him if they saw his truck at her house in the middle of the night. But apparently there were some things more important to Griffin than people possibly making incorrect assumptions. She appreciated his concern for both her safety and reputation.

"Maybe we could watch a short episode? I was right in the middle of a crime show earlier..." Bre began.

He laughed. "You want to watch a crime show after all that?"

She shrugged. "At least it makes me feel like I'm not the only one?"

Without any more argument, he left the dogs on the couch with her and headed to her kitchen. "Do you have popcorn, at least?"

"Cabinet above the stove," she confirmed. She petted Ember and Flapjack behind the ears, enjoying the kisses they slathered on her cheeks as her reward.

Griffin came back in and shook his head. "They really did take my seat."

"You could always ask them to get down and have it back," she said in a move of uncharacteristic boldness. It felt like her veins were buzzing with nervousness and maybe anticipation. She'd promised herself she wouldn't fall for him again, or admit that she'd never stopped falling for him, but wasn't he proving that her fears were unfounded?

She'd thought he'd abandoned her when he'd left town and holed up in his cabin, but he was just protecting himself. At this moment, when it mattered, he was there. Sure, he'd said at first he wouldn't help her search, but he was, and he was here now.

It was the opposite of what she'd grown up with. Parents who'd promised they'd make her next elementary Christmas concert and then never showed. When she'd gotten home after her first-grade concert—a friend's mom had dropped her at their small shack of a house—they'd both been passed out on the floor, and Ben had been crying. "I tried to wake them up for your concert. I wanted to see it." She'd wrapped her brother in her arms and they'd both wept for the childhood they'd wanted, could picture, and for some reason could not have.

This wasn't like that. Griffin resisted making promises to her, but when it came down it, he was there for her.

That's what she reminded herself of as he settled next to her on the couch, close enough their shoulders were touching.

He started the show and she felt herself relaxing into him. She looked his direction once, but he was so much closer than she'd realized that she looked away, heart pounding.

The show ended too soon and Griffin stood. "I'd better let you try to sleep."

"You're leaving?"

He reached over and brushed her hair behind her ear. Bre found herself wishing he would do it again or hold her hand. Anything that meant he was closer to her.

"You need to sleep."

"I don't see how I can," she said seriously. "I was down here on the couch because I already couldn't sleep and wanted to make sure I heard it if anyone came into the house."

"So sleep down here again." He moved the sofa pillows back to one end. "Lie down right here…"

She did so, wordlessly. Griffin took the blanket she'd shoved to the floor and laid it across her. "Flapjack, up," he told the dog, who immediately jumped onto the couch and curled up on her feet.

"I thought I'd leave him with you."

The tension in her shoulders relaxed and Bre took a deep breath. "Okay."

"Not going to argue?"

"I never argue when someone tries to give me a dog, even temporarily. It's as rule of mine," she said with a small smile.

"You'll be safer with him than you are alone."

Bre nodded and thanked him, aware he was trying not to worry as he and Ember headed to the front door.

Surprisingly she found herself relaxing into the cushions. Maybe she could sleep again.

And maybe Griffin's words were true about him too. Maybe she was safer with him, even emotionally, than she was alone.

NINE

When Griffin opened his eyes in the morning, they felt like sandpaper, dry and tired, from a night with more waking hours than sleeping. He stretched his arms out and tried to stretch his legs to the best of his ability, but the driver's seat of his truck didn't offer a lot of room.

Beside him, on the passenger seat, Ember stretched, too, and sighed. Neither of them had slept well.

He opened the truck door and climbed out, relishing the feeling of unfolding his limbs. Sleeping in her driveway had seemed like such a good idea and, in some ways, it had been. Bre didn't need to be entirely alone, but he hadn't wanted to sleep inside the house, lest anyone assume something was happening that wasn't. He wanted to protect her reputation but also keep her safe. This was the next best option to being inside, as it allowed him to keep an eye on the perimeter, and at least have a part in trying to prevent her from coming to further harm.

Ember followed him up to the front step and Griffin knocked on the door. He heard nothing inside the house. More than likely, Bre had been asleep and it would take her a minute to wake, hear the knocking, walk to the door… Still, he was uneasy. He knocked again.

Bre opened the door, her blond hair still in tangles like she'd slept on it. "Sorry, I didn't hear you. I hope you weren't waiting a long time." She moved back for him to enter, and reached to pet Ember as soon as the dog walked in the door.

"Only a minute. How did you sleep?" Griffin asked as he stepped inside and locked the door behind him.

"It was one of the best nights of sleep I've had." She shook her head. "Apparently, I should have borrowed a dog a long time ago. Want some coffee?" She started toward the kitchen before he answered, and Griffin followed her.

"Why don't you let me make it? You're barely awake." He didn't wait for an answer, but walked into her kitchen and quickly found what he was looking for.

"Can I ask you a question?" Bre asked from where she'd perched on one of the stools at her breakfast counter.

Griffin looked over at her. Even half asleep, she was beautiful, blond hair tangled over her shoulders. "Sure." *Anything*, he'd have said if he hadn't caught himself.

"Why doesn't the chief want me searching?"

He pressed the button on the grinder to grind their coffee and thought about it while the machine whirred and prepped the coffee grounds. "He let you search, right? So are you asking why he wouldn't let you do more, beyond the conflict of interest? You're the one who knows the answer to that, Bre," he finally said. "You've trained for years, worked as a police officer, and you're the one equipped to solve this case."

She snorted. "If only other people thought so."

"Your boss doesn't agree?"

Bre shrugged. "He let me continue to investigate at

Get up to 4 FREE FABULOUS BOOKS in your welcome box!

To thank you for being a loyal reader we'd like to send you up to 4 FREE BOOKS, absolutely free when you try the Harlequin Reader Service.

Just write "YES" on the Loyal Reader Voucher and we'll send you your welcome box with 2 free books from each series you choose plus free mystery gifts! Each welcome box is worth over $20.

Try **Love Inspired® Romance Larger-Print** and get 2 books and fall in love with inspirational romances that take you on an uplifting journey of faith, forgiveness and hope.

Try **Love Inspired® Suspense Larger-Print** and get 2 books where courage and optimism unite in stories of faith and love in the face of danger.

Or **TRY BOTH and get 2 books from each series!**

Your welcome box is completely free, even the shipping! If you continue with your subscription, you can look forward to curated monthly shipments of brand-new books from your selected series, always at a discount off the cover price! Plus you can cancel any time.

So don't miss out, return your Loyal Readers Voucher today to get your Free Welcome Box.

Pam Powers

LOYAL READER
FREE BOOKS VOUCHER
WELCOME BOX

YES! I Love Reading, please send me a welcome box with up to 4 FREE BOOKS and Free Mystery Gifts from the series I select.

Just write in "YES" on the dotted line below then return this card today and we'll send your welcome box asap!

→ — YES — ←

Which do you prefer?

☐ **Love Inspired®**
Romance
Larger-Print
122/322 IDL GRET

☐ **Love Inspired®**
Suspense
Larger-Print
107/307 IDL GRET

☐ **BOTH**
122/322 & 107/307
IDL GRE5

FIRST NAME

LAST NAME

ADDRESS

APT.#

CITY

STATE/PROV.

ZIP/POSTAL CODE

EMAIL ☐ Please check this box if you would like to receive newsletters and promotional emails from Harlequin Enterprises ULC and its affiliates. You can unsubscribe anytime.

LI/LIS-622-LR_LRV22

HARLEQUIN® Reader Service —Here's how it works:

▲ If offer card is missing write to: Harlequin Reader Service, P.O. Box 1341, Buffalo, NY 14240-8531 or visit www.ReaderService.com ▲

BUSINESS REPLY MAIL
FIRST-CLASS MAIL   PERMIT NO. 717   BUFFALO, NY

POSTAGE WILL BE PAID BY ADDRESSEE

HARLEQUIN READER SERVICE
PO BOX 1341
BUFFALO NY 14240-8571

NO POSTAGE
NECESSARY
IF MAILED
IN THE
UNITED STATES

the pass, which I appreciated. I was technically working yesterday and he had no problem with me spending the entire day searching for my niece."

"But?"

"I'm not sure he actually thinks I can do it on my own."

"You probably can't do it on your own."

She blinked at him a few times and finally shook her head. "Remind me not to come to you when I need a pep talk. Your pregame speech needs some work, Griffin."

"That's not what I mean. If anyone *could* do it alone, it would be you. But you've got a whole department, right? And the FBI. People who are good at different things…"

"The department is stretched thin. There are a few officers on the search still, but I don't know how many resources the chief can direct toward it."

"Call him and ask." He added the coffee to the French press he'd found in the closet.

"Not a bad idea." She reached for her phone and walked out of the room. He could hear the conversation in the next room, but just barely. Judging by her tone, though, it was going fairly well.

She walked back in and smiled at Griffin.

"You were right. He's not giving up. He told me I should take today off, but that if I didn't, I should use whatever department resources I need within reason to get a game plan together. He's sending the crime scene team over in a little while to process…well, my house, after last night."

"That is great news. Finally, more movement, right?"

"And then yesterday…" She hesitated. They'd barely

had a chance to discuss the scent the dogs had found. "We had so much progress but..."

"But what? The fact that someone broke into your house last night just confirms we made great progress."

"I still don't understand—why Addy? Why doesn't he want us to find her?"

"Stop looking for answers, Bre. He's a serial killer. Look for Addy instead. He doesn't want you to find her because, when he hunts, his victims always die. He doesn't want her to be any different."

"So you think she's already hurt?" Her voice was edged with panic and he knew he'd made a misstep.

"I don't know. I hope not."

She didn't look terribly comforted, and Griffin couldn't blame her. After frowning at him for at least thirty seconds, she finally changed the subject.

"How did you get here so early, by the way?"

"I slept in the driveway, in my truck, but anyway..." His words trailed off, but he couldn't help but notice the way she was looking at him, like he was too good to be true. Then, just as quickly, that expression vanished and her usual more guarded expression was in its place.

"He's a hunter, right? And these women are his quarry. What if he views Addy that way? Maybe he's hurt her already, like he shot you today, and he's tracking her to try to..." Griffin found the words hard to say.

"To try to kill her, once and for all."

"And that's why he's following you, to have you lead him to her."

"That might be why, but he's also trying to get rid of me. That's something he's never done before, hunted outside of the pass."

"Do you think that will change the FBI's assessment of him? Is he changing his MO?"

Bre was shaking her head. "No. I think this is a one-time thing. I just don't know he cares so much about stopping me."

"He can't risk you finding her first."

"But why?"

Griffin met Bre's eyes. "What if...what if you finding her means that somehow you find out who he is and his days of terrorizing people are over?"

"Listen, I know it's a terrible thing for a police officer to say, but bringing a murderer to justice isn't even my main goal right now. It would be nice but, first of all, this has been going on for a long time, and I'm not cocky enough to think I can end it all on my own. Also, what I want, *all* I want, is to get Addy back safe. Whether he gets away or not doesn't matter. Not really."

It was a step for her, Griffin knew, because Bre liked to be the best at everything. Competitive to a fault, she planned her actions out, and she never let the bad guy win. That was one reason he hadn't been surprised she'd decided to go into law enforcement. And she loved her niece that much.

"I don't think you have a choice. It's you or him, Bre. He's decided that, and everything about his behavior says so."

She'd undergone police training to read people, as well, and to predict their behavior, though she knew she wasn't an FBI profiler. As he handed her a mug of French-pressed coffee, he saw her consider his words and then finally nod.

"You're probably right."

"So there's only one choice to make," he stated. Her forehead creased in a slight frown. "You've got to figure out where else we should be searching and let's get a plan together."

She grinned up at him and his heart skipped. He wanted more than anything to find Addy, to be the kind of hero both Bre and Addy deserved to have. The kind of man Ben would have been—had he lived.

But a killer wanted her dead.

And Griffin was no hero, much as he might want to be. He could only hope he could do enough to help. Before more people ended up on the wrong side of an arrow.

When he'd suggested that Bre start planning where they should search next, Griffin hadn't anticipated that it would start raining. That virtually destroyed their chances of a successful search today. The rain hid the scents in the area and made searching more difficult. Part of him was relieved, because he felt Bre needed a day to rest, but the other part of him felt time running out for Addy, something that was unacceptable to him. She was his best friend's daughter, and if that wasn't reason enough to fuel his urgency, the fact that she was part of Bre's immediate family now certainly was. Maybe he was a hopeless romantic somewhere down inside his cynical self, because he couldn't help but hope that one day the three of them would be sitting down to dinner, as a family, with all of this behind them.

Three people who had experienced brokenness in different ways. But not beaten.

Griffin needed to find her.

He didn't care if the dogs couldn't help him; if he had to, he would go out by himself.

"So, if we found her scent here…" Bre pointed to one of the maps Griffin had brought inside with him. It was lying on the coffee table, next to a jar of peanut butter and a couple of spoons, which they'd eaten for breakfast, along with a couple of apples. "She should be in one of these locations." She'd highlighted where they'd found the scrap from her jacket several days before and some surrounding areas.

"Or she could be over here." Griffin highlighted the next ridgeline over on the map. "Sometimes scent can travel like that."

"But we found the cloth down on the slope."

"All that means is she was down there at some point. It doesn't mean she stayed in one place."

Bre looked at the map and frowned. "Okay, we won't rule that out yet."

"What if I went back alone today, and you stayed here to work on the research side. It would be really useful."

"You're trying to convince a cop to pick desk duty? You've got to be kidding." Bre laughed and shook her head. "If anyone's going up there today, it should be me."

"We have to stay together when we search, so it doesn't go any faster with two of us. You said the chief said you could use resources. What kinds of things would you look at if this were any missing person?"

Bre frowned and shook her head. "It's hard for me to look at it objectively."

"Your boss would say that means you shouldn't be on this case," he reminded her gently. "I've worked with police departments before. This is a pretty big conflict of interest."

"I'm not going to stop looking." She stood, walked toward the living room, blew out a breath, then walked back.

"First, I would pursue the search on the ground," she finally said, and he noticed her tone had changed. It was more confident, less room for frustration in it. "That's where the priority has to be."

"I'm not leaving you out of that. I'm suggesting we divide and conquer, just for today."

"It has nothing to do with my arm, right?" She raised her eyebrows, her expression challenging him.

Exasperation built in him, but he worked to control it. Bre was her own person; she'd been functionally independent years earlier than most people were, definitely before high school, though she'd lived in foster homes up through graduation. Sure her foster families had been fine, they'd taken care of her in some ways, but she'd made all her own major decisions and had never really functioned as anything but someone who was independent. Or at the most, independent along with her brother. Griffin wished she was used to people caring for her, enough that she didn't bristle every time someone tried to.

'Course he'd said that to Ben, *last time they'd been close. Don't try to protect her, Griffin. She doesn't need someone treating her like she's fragile, or she'll feel like she is.*

It had made sense in theory. It was different to be in a situation like this and feel like his friend must have been wrong about his little sister.

"Maybe it has a little to do with your arm," he started,

trying to ignore the flash of triumph on Bre's face, "but there's nothing wrong with me wanting to make sure you're feeling okay. And I really think that we need a plan. We can just keep going out in the pass and following the scent trail, but we may need every resource we can get. Who saw her the day she disappeared? Has that lead been followed?"

She seemed to be considering it. Griffin waited, holding his breath.

"Fine." Bre exhaled, wishing getting rid of all of her frustration was as easy as pushing out a breath. "You go search today. Try to see if you can eliminate these areas." She made some gestures at the map.

"You got it."

Her arm was throbbing and as much as she would have preferred to be included in the search, she knew Griffin was right. They couldn't keep aimlessly hiking around the pass, they needed more of a plan than that. He could go do another random canvas today, but it would be helpful if Bre could put some of her investigative training to work and develop something a little more specific for them to use as a game plan.

Still, it was hard to watch him pack up and load up Ember.

"You're sure you don't want to take him too?" She motioned to Flapjack, who was chewing on a carrot at her feet. She didn't have dog treats, but when she'd gone to get a snack out of the fridge, he'd sat beside her and looked longingly at what must have appeared to him to be a magic food box, so she'd felt sorry for him. She didn't have any bones or anything particularly canine friendly, but had figured carrots were shaped enough like bones they could work.

He seemed happy enough with his prize.

"No, keep him with you. Wait just a second." He hurried to the truck and jogged back with a bag of dog food. "Here's something for him. I'll see you later. Lock this behind me." He nodded to the door and then pulled it shut behind himself. She locked it, and he was gone.

She was relieved he'd left Flapjack and probably hadn't been as good at hiding it as intended. Having someone break in and try to shoot her had shaken her. She'd worked with crime out *there* before, but not here, in her house. The invasion of privacy made her insides squirm. The dog helped her to feel less alone, like she'd have someone on her side should the killer come back to finish what he'd started.

As she thought of him, the wound on her arm throbbed.

The doorbell rang then and Bre flinched. Flapjack's ears perked, but nothing in his demeanor indicated that she was in danger, so she moved to the door and opened it.

It was the chief.

"Come in." She motioned for him to enter and he did so. Two officers entered behind him. Officer Kraft and Officer Kerley, both with the Wolf River Police Department.

It was strange to think of her own house as a crime scene, but it was by far not the strangest concept she'd had to grapple with this week. She pointed them in the direction of the garage door, where she was fairly sure the intruder had entered the house.

"Did you come to look at the crime scene too?" she finally asked the chief.

"No, I came to talk to you."

His tone was more serious than usual. Bre motioned to the empty chair in her living room and the chief took a seat. Bre sat on the couch.

"You get a dog?"

"This is Flapjack. He's on loan from Griffin."

"Good idea." He looked troubled and Bre couldn't take the suspense anymore. He'd found out something, she was almost sure of it.

"Is it Addy? Did you find…" She choked on the unfinished question.

He shook his head immediately. "No. I still have several men in the pass, but no substantial progress. I'm hoping Griffin and his dog are able to find something."

"They went back out but I stayed here today."

"Good." He nodded. "Listen, Bre, I don't know how to say this without beating around the bush, and you know I don't like to do that."

"Okay." Her pulse was accelerating, her heart in her throat.

"I'm going to have to put you on a leave of absence if you continue to work with Griffin. This is a strange situation. I thought you might be able to work on it on your days off and still be available on workdays, but it's not aboveboard that way."

Her shoulders relaxed. "Is that all?"

"That's the worst of it."

"No problem."

"It's unpaid leave."

"I can make it work." She'd expected bad news and this wasn't ideal—she'd have to go into her savings—

but it wasn't terrible. She also wouldn't have access to all the resources she'd hoped to have if she wasn't working the case out of the office, but it did give her far more flexibility. Truth be told, she wasn't able to focus on anything else right now besides Addy, so the idea of being able to do that without worrying about her job was appealing.

"Can you still share information with me, even though what I'm doing is purely on my own time?"

"Yes. I don't see why that would be a problem."

"Have they finished processing Addy's car yet?" The plan had been to take it into the department, to one of the large garages that served as an evidence bay, and examine the contents for anything that could help their investigation.

"Should be a couple more days. We're stretched thin."

"And the FBI? Any progress there?"

Bre noticed as the chief shook his head that he looked like he'd aged just in the last week. His hair looked a little grayer and there were more lines around his eyes. She probably looked like she had visibly grown a bit older too. "The FBI is still working on their profile, trying to approach this like it's some kind of math. Probabilities and profiles…"

The chief was old school, Bre knew, from when more of the police work was done by hand, gut instinct, or other ways than computer systems.

"And? Any changes?"

"They think it's a first responder."

TEN

Her breath caught and Bre had to take an intentionally deep inhale and then let it out slowly. "A police officer?"

"Not necessarily. They said it *could* be a police officer, but it could be any other number of people who have involvement in this case or other similar cases. EMTs."

Bre thought of how she'd been alone in the house with the EMTs, how easy it could have been for one of them to finish the job the intruder had started. Had one of them *been* the intruder?

"Or a firefighter."

"There aren't any of those on this case," she reminded him.

"True, but they still are trained in similar ways. The person killing women in the pass—" Bre knew the chief disliked the nickname "the Echo Pass Hunter" as he thought it gave too much notoriety "—knows how first responders work. He thinks like us. Methodical, intentional, with his own version of protocol. He operates like us."

But the idea that someone on the inside could be guilty...that someone could help with the search, be at the update meetings, and be the one with blood on his hands...

Bre shivered.

"Or…" The chief took a weighted breath. "It could be a search-and-rescue worker."

"It's not Griffin," Bre said immediately.

"I'm just telling you what they said. We have to investigate all of the local candidates."

"We need a list of everyone who has been present at any point who fits the description of a first responder. Are we thinking it could be a volunteer too?"

When Addy had first gone missing, some people had volunteered to help search and been paired, for the most part, with law enforcement, due to the risk level involved in the pass. As it became clear with time that this was a criminal situation and a bad actor could still be in the pass, posing a risk to searchers, volunteers had been less utilized.

"Possibly." He ran a hand through his thinning hair. "I don't want you to see a killer in every person you encounter, but—"

"But I need to," Bre said.

He nodded.

"Thanks for telling me. And telling me in person." She let out a breath. This would have been too much to take in over the phone.

"I'm not going to stop looking for her. She's a good kid, Bre. She deserves every chance she can get."

"Thanks, Chief."

"You keep looking too. Your job isn't in danger, if that's a worry. I just can't have you spending all your time on this with the amount of freedom you need and keep you on my list of on duty officers. Plus, I know you're not taking any actual time off, which would violate policy also."

He seemed to feel bad still, but Bre actually saw the blessing in disguise that this was. "It's okay."

"Find her, Bre."

"I'm doing my best." She swallowed against the lump in her throat, tried to hold back tears for the millionth time this week. "Tell me when you have an update on the car?"

"I will. Call if you haven't heard from me by day after tomorrow."

He stood then, mumbled something about checking on how the crime scene team was doing, and walked out of the room. Bre just sat there, trying to sort through everything he'd said.

She wasn't working right now. It was odd that would be a bother in light of the fact her niece was missing, but she did want to use all the time she could possibly use to find Addy. Being a police officer was part of who she was, maybe even the best part. How did she just let that go right now?

It was too much for her brain to work on. Instead, she decided to focus on what Griffin had suggested, looking at the map for places that seemed most likely to yield something in a search.

Several areas had been ruled out. But what if Addy had been running in the pass and circled back? It wasn't impossible.

The vastness of the pass, overwhelming when you were in it, was almost more overwhelming on paper. Huge, vast expanses of wilderness were reduced to a square inch, and Bre knew that finding Addy would be worse than locating a needle in a haystack. A person alone in the Alaskan wilderness was an even more terrifying, hopeless proposition.

She worked until there was nothing else to do with the map, then took to pacing around the house. After a little while of pacing, she started calling Addy's friends and talking to them, making sure she hadn't made any new friends lately, or had plans to hike the pass with anyone Bre didn't know about. That line of investigation yielded nothing. Then she sat and made a list of all the first responders working in town that she knew of, using the internet to fill in some gaps in her own knowledge. Then there was nothing else to do, and she was back to pacing. She hated waiting. She should have gone with Griffin to search today. But even as she told herself that, her arm throbbed and she knew she would have been a liability.

She applied more of the Neosporin to her wound, and laid down, thinking as she did about Addy's friends and who she hadn't called. There had to be someone...

There wasn't. Bre had chased every lead there was at this point and, while she might be discouraged because]she felt like she wasn't doing enough, the fact was that she was doing everything she possibly could.

Frustration building, she walked into the kitchen, then into the mudroom where the officers were still working on processing the scene. It looked to Bre like her would-be killer had forced open the mudroom door. She'd already made plans to have it repaired as soon as possible with a more secure door.

"Finding anything good?" she asked Officer Kraft, who was bent down, trying to lift a footprint off the floor's surface.

"I'm almost done." He finished his work and then stood to talk to her. "I found a couple good footprints, some organic matter that is probably pretty unhelpful as we don't have any kinds of distinguishing plant material around here."

"Which is a shame," Bre said with a smile. "In procedural shows, the bad guy always steps in some kind of obscure plant that can only be traced to one location and they crack the whole case."

"If only, right?" Officer Kraft shook his head. "But the prints are good. Looks like some kind of hiking shoe, which up here doesn't narrow it down too much. They're men's shoes, size twelve. No fingerprints on the doorknob coming in, looks like he used a shirt or something to cover his hands, but I think I found some partials here." He motioned to the doorway from the mudroom to the kitchen. "It's possible he grabbed it without thinking. Or it's possible they're your prints. But I'm hopeful. They're a little higher than where you would naturally grab, which fits with what I'm assuming his height would be, based on his shoe size."

"That's fantastic. How long before we get those results back?"

He made a face and shook his head. "Watkins is out of town. He's supposed to be back in a couple of days, but said he could come back tomorrow if we need him to."

"So there's going to be a bit of a wait before we even know if it's our guy."

"Right. But I'll tell him we do need him tomorrow."

Still, it was a glimmer of hope, and Bre would take it. She couldn't believe the Hunter could possibly have been sloppy enough to leave any fingerprints, but then again, most of his crimes had taken place outside, in areas that were impossible to obtain such physical evidence. If that had made him careless, Bre would take it.

Anything that could help them. She wished they could find out today whether they'd actually gotten his prints, and if they were in the system, but tomorrow wasn't bad.

"Thanks."

"You really doing okay?"

They weren't close friends or anything, but they'd worked together before and Bre considered him a work friend. One she could be fairly honest with. She made a face. "I've been better."

"Pretty hardcore, what you've been through and survived."

"Not much of a choice, right? The alternative isn't something I'm in a hurry to rush."

He laughed. "Sure. Gotta stay above ground for now."

"That's the goal."

They laughed about death and danger, because what else could you do when you faced it so often in your job?

He packed up his gear and the samples and then opened the garage door. Officer Kerley was finishing up outside, having printed those doors and frames.

"Anything out here?"

"Some." He shrugged. "We'll see."

"I wish I knew how to thank you guys," she said, suddenly feeling the lack of sleep from last night. Her arm was throbbing. She had never realized the sense of indebtedness you could feel to someone who was trying to remove terror from of your life. The exclamations of gratitude she'd heard over the years when she'd been able to do the same for others made more sense now.

"Find that girl," Kraft said with a smile. "That's all the thanks we need."

"That's the plan," Bre said, hoping this one would work out.

She stayed outside until they'd driven away, standing for a minute in the cool air, enjoying the sun warming her. Then she shivered, feeling almost like someone was watching. Surely, whomever had broken in wouldn't still be there? She imagined him, in the trees somewhere across the street, watching the police process the scene.

Was Bre in his bow sight?

She eased the door open, shut it hard behind her and locked it. It wasn't worth the risk of being outside. Griffin had been right.

There was nothing else to do with the map. She knew exactly where she wanted to investigate next. For now, she'd lie on the couch and see if she could take a nap. Because as soon as Griffin came back, Bre was going to try to talk him into going back out again. Together.

Much to Griffin's surprise, it hadn't rained much in the pass. But to his frustration, Ember still hadn't been able to find Addy's scent at all. It had been a few hours before he'd finally decided to check back in with Bre to see what areas on the map she thought might be most likely. He tried his phone but didn't have service, so he headed back down, marking his GPS location so he could add this area to the map and update the parts of it they'd had a chance to clear.

He hurried to his truck once they were down, and drove to Bre's house, not relaxing until he saw that it looked the same as when he had left. The doors were shut, nothing looked disturbed.

Still, after last night, tension was high. He hurried to the front door and knocked.

Bre opened it. Okay.

He let out a long breath.

"What?" Her voice sounded as anxious as he felt. "Are you okay?"

"I was just worried about you. Can I come in?"

"Sure. But I was hoping we could go right back out." She stepped back so he had room to enter, and he shut the door behind them, locking it.

"Why?"

A grin had spread across her face. "Because I think I have an idea about where Addy might be."

"Get your gear and Flapjack. We can leave right now."

Bre nodded and hurried off.

He hadn't wanted her out with her arm hurt, but if she thought she might have figured out where Addy could be, then it was worth having her there, even with an injury. She lost no time hurrying around, packing a backpack with hiking gear and a few snacks.

"Could you get a bag of dog food too? I don't mind carrying it, but I didn't plan to be out as late as we're going to be and they may need dinner."

She did so and he packed it away.

"How long can we search?" she asked as they walked to the truck. Griffin noticed that Bre didn't look at him when she talked, but kept her eyes on the trees across the street, scanning back and forth.

"Did something happen today?"

"No." She answered without looking at him.

"You're looking for something in the woods."

They both climbed into the truck, shutting the doors behind them. Griffin put the car in drive and started to move it forward, and then Bre looked over at him.

"I just…" She shook her head. "I stepped outside today, just for a minute, to watch the officers who were here processing the scene for prints and DNA, and I stayed out there for a minute, literally a minute, after they left."

"And?" He kept driving.

"I thought I sensed something." Her voice had lowered, whether she'd done so intentionally or not. "Like someone watching me. You don't think he really is, do you?"

Griffin didn't know what to think at this point. Serial killers made no sense to him, and this one made even less sense than those he'd seen on TV. Stalking seemed awfully personal… But at the same time, the Echo Pass Hunter seemed determined to remove Bre from the picture.

It seemed that Bre took Griffin's silence as an answer, which was fair.

"I'll be more careful," she promised without being asked.

"Good." He hesitated, reached for her hand and squeezed it quickly then let it go. "I don't want anything to happen to you." It was hard to keep his voice steady on the last sentence. He hadn't actually expected to be so affected by squeezing her hand, but he had been. Touching her was comfortable and confusing. Easy and intense. The longer they worked together on this case, the more Griffin wondered what would have happened if he hadn't left to be something of a hermit after failing to find Megan alive. Would he and Bre still be in a relationship?

Married?

Was this God's way of giving him another chance

with her? If it was, he was extremely thankful for it and mentally whispered a prayer of thanks to tell Him so. This time he'd try not to mess it up.

Griffin looked over at her and, for half a second, Griffin almost thought Bre could read his mind. She was looking at him as though she'd felt like something had slipped away too. He wanted to reach for her hand again and not let go this time, but didn't quite have the courage to do it. They'd been friends, then apart, for too long, and it had been an enormous risk to try to start a romantic relationship the *first* time. Surely, he couldn't try again without consequences to the friendship they'd only just scraped back together.

Besides, she deserved better than Griffin. He was the one who had messed things up before; who was to say he wouldn't do it again? And Bre had been hurt too much already.

So instead, he smiled at her with what he hoped was a friendly smile. Low key.

Then he looked at the road and tried to remember what he was doing. Search. Dogs. Addy.

"Where do you want to go when we get there?" he asked.

"Back where we were the other day."

"I went there this morning." Griffin thought she'd meant she had somewhere new she wanted to search. Disappointment threatened to discourage him even more than he was already as he pulled into the parking lot.

"Look." She pulled out the map and pointed. "This is where they dogs caught the scent the other day, right?"

Once he was parked and had shut the truck off, he

glanced over. "I can double check the GPS coordinates, but yes, pretty close to there."

"Where did you search today?"

Griffin motioned to the north side of the area and looked up at Bre, who was grinning. "I think I remembered something that will help. There's a boulder in this direction. Addy and I have hiked this way before. It's its own trail, but you access it from Sunrise Ridge. I don't know where it leads, but there's a good chance if she's moving around on her own, she would go there."

Bent over, he continued to study the map, to make sure he understood where Bre was telling them they needed to look. What she was saying made sense. It also fit with the search profile he'd come up with for Addy. A teenage girl who was in any kind of danger was more likely to seek out familiar locations for comfort, which would also give them a perceived advantage. If there was a trail she'd hiked more often, chances were good she might be on it.

They climbed out of the truck and readied themselves. Griffin had expected that Ember might be tired, but she seemed to have just as much energy as she had earlier. Flapjack also seemed eager to have his own chance at working.

The sun was falling behind a cloud, and while they still had hours of daylight left, a glance at his watch told Griffin it was four in the afternoon, far later than he preferred to start a search, when he had a chance. The beginnings of twilight seemed to linger, and then the dim light—not quite black, but too dark to search— would come all at once. He felt something in his stomach. Unease? Anticipation?

"You're sure you're up for going out here again? After what happened last time?"

"If you don't think I'm willing to take whatever risks I have to, to find my niece, you don't know me at all," Bre said as she pulled on her backpack.

That was the problem. Griffin *did* know her, and he knew she would take whatever risks were necessary. He didn't blame her; he wanted Addy found too.

He just hoped he would be able to keep both her and Bre safe.

ELEVEN

The next few hours were full of highs and lows. One of the dogs would get the scent and then lose it. Griffin was about to suggest they try again in the morning when Ember's ears perked up, and she ran back to Griffin, excited. Flapjack did the same.

"She's got it again," he said in a low voice.

They hurried after her. Ember was even more focused this time, driven, it seemed, toward whatever she smelled.

"And it's Addy for sure?" she confirmed with Griffin, who nodded.

"Yes."

He was serious, and Bre didn't want to ask anything else. Was he concerned her niece might not be alive? He hadn't given her all the details of the way the search dogs were capable of alerting to different things, so she couldn't say for sure, but Bre didn't think so that was his current worry. This felt good. Like maybe this time they would actually find her after so many times that they'd come close and still walked away empty-handed. She didn't have a reason to believe this might be the time, except for a little flicker of hope inside her.

It had been too many days, Bre knew, to expect her niece to be alive. If she was running from the Echo Pass Hunter, she might not be able to get to water, especially if she felt like she had to hide out. People only had three days without water, she recalled clearly from several backcountry skills classes she'd been in.

But Bre wasn't going to let go of the possibility.

They moved quickly through the trees, following the narrow path the K-9s were taking. It wasn't a popular hiking trail, Bre didn't think, because it didn't seem well trodden. But the scent seemed to be thick here, judging by Ember's behavior and the way she was actively sniffing the air.

A glance over at Griffin confirmed it for her. He was grinning.

Did that mean he was starting to believe her when she told him that he did have what it took and he hadn't failed years ago? After their argument about it the other night, she hadn't brought it up again, as much as she'd wanted to.

They'd just reached a spot on the steep slope that had started to flatten out a little when a sharp crack tore through the air, the sound reverberating off the mountains that rimmed the pass.

"Gunshot, get down!" she yelled to Griffin, grabbing his arm and pulling him with her. They hit the dirt with a thud and Bre rolled immediately onto her stomach to look around to try to figure out where the shots had come from.

"Over there." She motioned to a spot up on the hillside where she'd caught a glint in the sunlight, probably the glass of a rifle's scope catching the light. "He's up on the hill." It was a good distance, five to six hundred yards. "Can the dogs smell whoever it is from that far away?"

"Hard to say, but they're not tracking bad actors. They're tracking Addy."

"And she's here somewhere." Bre's eyes widened, the shooting scaring her even more. What if they'd led danger right to her niece? Without thinking, she started to sit up, look around.

Griffin pulled her back down. The next volley of shots was even closer to them and she sent him a look of thanks.

"We've got to move," he said.

"How though? There's not really a trail and the brush is so low we'll have to practically crawl"

"Follow me."

She watched as he kept himself pressed to the ground and moved into the trees.

Bre secretly wondered if they were going to escape from a killer only to run into a bear who was equally likely to hurt them. But at the moment she had no other options, so she followed Griffin. The dogs did, too, and unless she was mistaken, Flapjack seemed to stick close to her. She reached for his head, petting him behind the ears to reassure herself that he was okay and that maybe they would be too.

The trees were thick and green, the ground cool underneath her hands as she crawled through alders and then, eventually, spruce trees. They were going down the mountain, toward the creek, if she understood where they were. She couldn't exactly pull out a map right now to confirm.

She knew Griffin would get them back to where they

needed to be. She had confidence in him, which should have alarmed her, but didn't.

The gunshots continued, though Bre thought they were managing to put distance between them and who-ever wanted to harm them.

"Bre," Griffin whispered and motioned for her to come closer to him. He pointed out a little hollow in the ground, maybe where a moose had made a bed, and the way the trees seemed to shelter it from view.

"It's as good a place as any. Let's stay put here. I think it's easier to defend ourselves if we are in one place."

She agreed and they climbed into the depression, people first then dogs. After the adrenaline rush of run-ning for her life, it felt overwhelming to be in one place. Still. And to be beside Griffin? She felt safe and cen-tered. Like she could finally take a breath.

"How long do you think we'll have to be here?" she asked after a few minutes of silence.

Griffin shrugged. "I don't know. What do you think? You're the cop."

"You're just as good about studying people."

He shrugged again, always noncommittal about his own abilities and talents. Maybe he really didn't know how good he was at some things, but Bre felt like he doubted himself more often than not. Despite every-thing they had gone through, he was one of the few people in this world she didn't doubt.

"I think he's getting frustrated. And desperate," she stated, thinking through all the pieces as she talked. "He's always used arrows and today he's hunting us with guns."

"Because he can use them from further away, I'm thinking."

Bre nodded. That was exactly where her mind had gone. "Because he's desperate to make us go away now. Before, he was still playing whatever his sick game is, but now he doesn't care if he follows his MO or anything. He just wants us dead."

"Why?" Griffin whispered back. "What does this guy have to lose with us being alive?"

"The security of not getting caught, for one thing. We've proved we aren't going to be scared off, no matter what he does. That can't bode well for him."

"Or," Griffin posited, "he didn't kill Addy and he's mad that didn't go according to plan."

She liked that idea, too, both because it made sense and gave her hope her niece could still be alive, and was impressed with Griffin's logic. "Or he has her and he's tying up loose ends."

"Nah. I don't like that one, there's no point."

"So you think this says she's alive?"

"Too hard to tell."

"What would she have done from where we caught her scent last? I know you can't have the dogs search like they normally would, but if she was really there…"

"She was—the dogs said so. Trust your dog. That's the number one rule of SAR handling."

"All right…" Bre continued. "Since she was there, we have a new starting point. What would she have done next?"

"It's too many variables, Bre. I can only make an educated guess."

"And yours is?"

"I think she'd be down here, near where there's water. Addy's a smart girl. She knows she needs to stay hydrated, and she wouldn't have been scared to go deeper into the wilderness if necessary with the skills she has. We may have lost the scent for now, but the dogs know they're not searching right now. We're hiding. There's a difference in my behavior, so there's a difference in theirs."

"But if we can search a—"

Gunshots again. These much louder and closer than before.

The caliber of bullet may have been different, too, Bre thought, but it was hard to tell from just the sound. Her training kicked in and this time Bre didn't hesitate or take the time to feel anything other than decisive.

"Come on." She took charge, leading them out of the range of the shooter. They'd been heading to the river, but the land opened up down there and they couldn't afford that kind of visibility right now. Instead, she doubled back on the path they had come, but far enough away from that trail that she hoped they'd stay hidden.

Was the shooter just aiming for the woods, hoping to flush them out, or could he actually see them? She wished there was a way to know, but it was impossible. Glancing back to make sure Griffin and the dogs were still following her, she continued on, back up the slope.

She wasn't going to die today, not without finding Addy. Her niece had too much ahead of her. Addy deserved a much better life than her dad and Bre had had. Bre had always done her best to make sure Addy got it, but she was going to redouble her efforts. And that started with getting Addy back.

They tore through the trees, quieter than Bre would have realized was possible. Something about the confident way the dogs moved soundlessly through the woods gave her the confidence to be discreet herself. She felt like she'd been made for this, right here.

If only Addy could see her now. For once, she didn't feel like she was playing by a careful rulebook, but was doing what needed to be done, thinking on her feet. Addy would be proud. Bre had to get her niece home safe, show her all she'd learned.

Lungs burning for air, Bre kept running until Griffin called out to her. She slowed and he motioned to a thick stand of spruce trees.

"I think we can stay under one of those for shelter if we need to."

What they needed to do was to get out of this pass and back into town, or better yet, find Addy, but neither was an option at the moment. It was too dangerous when the killer kept hunting them and kept getting closer.

She bent and climbed into the small depression under the spruce tree. Her heart was pounding, and when she brushed her hair behind her ear, she noticed she was sweating. Running through the woods had been exhausting.

"Do you think he's finally gone?" She turned to Griffin. He was closer than she'd realized and she found herself blinking in surprise as her breath caught in her chest. He was not a small man, and his broad shoulders always made her think of security. But this close? Griffin felt anything but safe, mostly because of the risk he presented to her heart. How many times could she fall for the same man? And at some point should she admit that she was probably never going to get over him?

"I don't think we can afford to assume it's safe."

His words were foreboding, for their situation now specifically and in general, but Bre knew he was right.

They *weren't* safe. Maybe wouldn't be for a long time. Today she felt entirely too conscious of that, too vulnerable, and it made her more scared than she could remember being in a long time.

Griffin was aware of every sound. How loud Flapjack's and Ember's breathing was, every shift he made that made his back scrape against the back of the spruce, every slight movement that rustled the tree limbs.

Anything could give them away and they couldn't run forever. Whoever was hunting them, and that felt like an apt description for it, had a massive advantage. Every time they were able to plot out where they wanted to be, play the offense. The hunter knew where his prey was and when he wanted to start shooting. Griffin and Bre had to react, never having a chance to be one step ahead. It made him feel powerless, an experience he would usually do everything possible to avoid feeling.

God, You're powerful, though. Help me to remember that with You on our side, we aren't weak or at any kind of disadvantage. You've got this. I need to remember that. Help me, please.

Beside him, he could sense Bre's tension. The last couple of hours had been a roller coaster, a microcosm of the last few days. The intense highs were matched by equally intense lows. When the dogs had alerted on Addy's scent again on this hike, Griffin had really thought today might be the day they found…something.

And they still could, but only if they were able to go out and continue searching; something now made too dangerous by the fact that they were caught in long game of cat and mouse.

"You doing okay?" he whispered and glanced over at

Bre. He thought she might look a little pale, but given how flushed she'd been a few minutes ago from running through the woods for their lives, maybe her face was just returning to its normal color.

"As well as I can be, I guess." She was petting Flapjack's smooth fur, and the dog looked like he was enjoying at least having a purpose sitting there helping her calm down, his face looking like he was almost smiling from the way his lips were stretched back, his body pressed against her leg.

"We're just going to have to stay put for a while and pray he doesn't shoot anymore."

He thought he felt her flinch beside him, but he couldn't decide if it had been intentional or not. Maybe because he'd mentioned praying? Or maybe he'd imagined the flinch altogether?

"If we're going to do that, why don't we just pray that God shows us where Addy is and be done with all of this?"

The flinching had been intentional, Griffin realized from the bitterness in her suggestion's tone. The idea of prayer was one that offended her... No, more than that, it had hurt her. But he didn't understand why.

"I have been praying for that," he finally said quietly, hoping that what the Bible said about a soft answer turning away wrath was true.

"It doesn't seem to be working yet."

"We haven't found her, but you don't know how much progress we've made. We could be close."

"And we might never find her. And you're sitting there talking about God, just like Addy would be."

There didn't seem to be a good response to that, and while Griffin's mind wanted to struggle for something to say, for a way to explain, or convince, he felt something in his spirit tell him to wait and be quiet. So he did. God could handle her on His own; it wasn't up to Griffin to argue her into faith.

They sat in silence for what had to be more than an hour. It felt right being here with Bre, and he prayed for her as they sat, silently, that one day she'd know Jesus and have the peace God seemed to be teaching him more about. It made him feel closer to God and to her and when Griffin finally checked his watch, two hours had passed. "I think we're safe now," he said as loudly as he dared.

"Do you think we should try to keep searching or walk back?" Griffin saw her glance up. It was approaching midnight and, while it was still light enough to move around, it would be difficult to see in another hour or so, especially with a sky as cloudy as today's had been.

"I'm not sure we should risk either one," he said honestly. "I've got some tarps to build shelters in my backpack. We could try that and just wait it out."

"Till morning?" She looked over at him, clearly still feeling their conversation from earlier, though he hadn't said another word about it. "I'm pretty sure we shouldn't be staying out all night together."

"My beliefs aren't about rules, Bre. It's more important that you're safe. Besides, we would sleep separately. Nothing is going to happen that would be anything wrong. Anything even approaching that would mean I wasn't acting in a way that valued you, and I wouldn't do that."

Her anger seemed to calm again, and when he looked back at her, he saw a tear shining in the dim light.

"Bre." He reached for her and she scooted closer to

him, finally burying her head in his chest as she sat beside him. His arm was around her, pulling her close, and she was sobbing.

"I want to find her. I want her to be okay and I don't understand how she could love God and this could happen. Ben followed God too. I never understood how he could believe when…".

"When he'd seen all that the two of you saw as kids?"

She looked up at him. Her makeup was smudged under her eyes, but Griffin still thought she was the most beautiful woman he'd ever seen.

God, if I'm not supposed to be attracted to her, I'm going to need a little help here, because she's beautiful outside, and even more so inside.

"You know about that?"

"It wasn't a secret that you were in foster care when we were in school." He dodged the question, but she caught it, as he should have been expecting.

"You know the details."

"Ben told me things." More things than he wanted to remember. "I understand why it would be difficult to believe a powerful God could have allowed some of it to happen." He knew of one story in particular that Ben had told him of when a stubborn Bre had refused to eat her dinner so they'd sent her to bed without any more food.

For three days. She'd had water, and nothing else.

When they'd told their caseworker, the foster parents had done a good job of pretending the situation was being twisted by Ben and Bre. But Griffin knew his friend, and he'd believed him.

He'd wrestled with it at the time himself, in high school, talking to his youth pastor several times about the classic question of how a good God could allow there to be evil in the world.

"It's more than difficult. It's impossible, at least for me."

But this time she didn't sound as angry. If anything, Griffin thought she sounded sad, and why wouldn't she? Bre had to know that his faith was the reason for his hope, for other people's hope, in the face of awful circumstances, but it clearly felt to her like it was out of her grasp.

"It's not impossible. We can talk about it whenever you want, but I'll let it go for now. But you need to know, it's not impossible."

"I will think about that," she said, leaning her head back against his chest. "This won't get you in some kind of Christian trouble, sitting close, right?"

He laughed softly. "No. It's okay. We're friends, Bre. That's allowed."

Silence again and, after a long stretch of it, Bre reached into her backpack and offered him a granola bar. He took it and they each ate one without talking.

"Remember that time it seemed like we might be more than friends?" Her voice was cautious, like she was tiptoeing up to a subject they'd both tried to leave in a dark corner of the conversational room the entirety of the last few days.

Were they really going to talk about this here and now? Yet, what else was there to do? There was nowhere to go, no way to run from it now, and it would be too exhausting to spend the entire night hiding out here and not addressing their onetime romance.

The upcoming conversation might scare him more

than the hunter waiting in the woods. Because it could go well.

That was scary.

Or it could go very, very wrong. He could lose her from his life forever.

That scared him more than any serial killer ever could.

TWELVE

"I definitely remember." His voice was deep and smooth. Bre's fear for her own safety has disappeared the moment Griffin had wrapped her in his arms while she'd cried. She felt safe with this man, always had since the time he was a boy.

She swallowed hard as she scooted away from him, just far enough to be able to look directly over at him again, instead of up at his face from where she'd laid her head on his chest. She was too scared to keep going, but too far into this conversation to back down now. He'd been trying to have it for almost a week, since he'd started helping her search, and she'd been dodging it. Now the moment of truth had come.

"What happened? I mean…do you know? I thought things… I thought we…" She was annoying herself with her inability to finish what she was saying. So she bit her lip to focus then spat the rest out. "I thought we had something and then you left. Did it not matter?"

Did *I* not matter? That was what she was really asking, whether he heard it or not. But Griffin knew her well enough, almost without her permission, that he probably knew what she was really asking.

"After Megan died, I felt awful. I felt like I should have been able to save her and I didn't. And I felt like it was my fault she died when I triggered that avalanche. Frankly, there was talk among a couple of people that it could have been negligence on my part, some kind of revenge since she and I had dated once."

Bre had known they had, and really, she wasn't surprised that he'd dated. He should have. He was an attractive man that any woman would like to be in a relationship with. That didn't mean it didn't hurt to think about him holding another woman in his arms though. She could be honest with herself about that.

"But you didn't, you wouldn't."

"I knew that." He shrugged. "Her family did too. But some people on the search team made comments, and I started to wonder if other people saw it that way too."

"Who were these people on the team who said that?" She didn't remember all his former coworkers that well, but she remembered the two he'd been close to. Don, who primarily worked support, helping with the, and Anna, whose dog had been a gorgeous German shepherd that specialized in water searches. Had it been one of them? She thought it had to have been to have affected him so much.

But he just shook his head at her question. "It doesn't matter. I was worried about how it would reflect on you You were just moving up in the police department, and you and I had just started to…"

"Date?"

"It sounds like such a shallow word for it, and we were never shallow."

Strange as it might have sounded, Bre knew exactly what he meant. They'd always shared a deep connection. Dating sounded so much easier and less weighty than what they'd had.

"I would have told you I didn't care what people said."

"I know. And I didn't want you making that sacrifice for me."

"So you just disappeared. For me." This was sounding familiar. How many times had people left in her life and then made excuses and tried to frame it like it was all Bre's fault, or worse, that they'd done it for her? Sometimes she didn't know what to believe anymore. Relationships were harder for her because of this, she knew. She hated that her past affected her so much. But it did.

"Not for you. That was part of my thinking," he admitted, reaching for her hand, "but I was also being selfish. And I was depressed."

His fingers, interwoven into hers, were making it hard to focus, but Bre liked it. "Like actually?"

He nodded. "I talked to a friend who is a counselor, did some work with him… I don't know how much it helped, and that wasn't his fault, it was mine."

It took her minute to process his words. Griffin didn't strike her as the kind of person who needed a counselor. When she looked at him, he was smiling.

"I know, it seemed weird to me too. But God…" he hesitated. "I'm not trying to push Him on you, Bre, but it's part of my story. Is that okay?"

She nodded.

"God really used it to help me see that while you were my first thought, I was my second thought. I didn't want to have to explain my failures to people over and over. I knew it wasn't intentional, but if people didn't believe me and it kept being brought up, I was going to have to keep facing it and I just… I couldn't. I didn't feel like I was strong enough. So I just went to my cabin and tried to leave there and go back into town as little as possible."

"You moved, except you didn't move," she commented. He'd had groceries delivered, she was pretty sure, along with other supplies, because it was extremely rare that anyone saw him in town.

"I just turned inward. I worked with the dogs, did training online to pay for mine and the dogs' food and whatever other things I needed…"

"So it wasn't because of me? You weren't trying to just end things?" She didn't know how to feel about that. Years lost, when they could have been in a happy relationship, because he'd felt guilty and crushed by what he'd perceived as his failure, which was really just an accident?

"It wasn't."

His voice sounded different ,and she looked over at him.

She blinked. "So where does that leave us?"

Griffin didn't answer immediately, but Bre thought she heard his breath catch in his throat and saw his Adam's apple bob as he swallowed.

He didn't answer her. He just moved forward, toward her, slowly, eyes on hers. Her lips parted as she realized he was going to kiss her if she didn't move, that he was giving her plenty of time to do so if the kiss wasn't what she wanted, if it wasn't the answer to the question that she was hoping for.

But it was.

Bre met him halfway, and he brushed his lips over hers. Taking his time, making up for lost time, Bre didn't know. All she knew was that this was right and good and exactly what she'd been missing in her life.

When he pulled back from the kiss, she didn't want him to go, but she understood.

"Does that answer your question?" he asked with the smallest hint of a smile.

"Yes," she whispered. "But it does bring up a few more."

"I have all the time in the world to talk at the moment." And for one minute, she forgot the heartbreaks she'd walked through and was still walking through, and just let herself enjoy a moment of peace.

"First question…" Bre started, looking like she was barely keeping a straight face. "Do you have anything else to eat?"

He had to muffle his own laughter. "No way that's really what you wanted to ask."

"Okay. No, it's not what I actually had in mind, but I really am hungry."

"If those questions will wait, then yes, I have some food in my backpack."

At the mention of food, Ember's ears perked up. His dogs were too smart for his own good sometimes. He opened the pack and pulled out the people food he had—a couple of sandwiches and some fruit leather—and treats and snacks for the animals as well. While each dog munched happily on a slice of salmon he'd packed, he handed Bre her food.

As night had fallen, it had gotten colder, so he also pulled out the survival blankets, thin foil rolls that unrolled into a space blanket that could keep a person warm.

"Thanks," Bre said, taking it and tucking it around

her shoulders as she shivered and then snuggled down into it.

"So," she said after a minute, "do you want to stay in Wolf River? Or do you have plans to move?"

"Going straight for the big questions first, huh?"

She shifted to where she could better meet his eyes, Griffin thought on purpose. "Why wouldn't I just go ahead and ask about the things that matter? This is my home and, more importantly for me, it's Addy's home. I can't leave."

She'd never been one to beat around the bush, which he appreciated about her.

"I'm planning to stay here." He didn't say that, even if he'd had plans to move, he'd have changed them for Bre and Addy; that seemed like it might scare her at the moment. She might be asking those kinds of questions, but he knew her. One kiss wasn't going to be enough to dispel all her fears about a relationship and make her jump in headfirst, not after the way he'd hurt her last time.

"Seriously, though, Griffin, what are we doing? Is this just a weird thing because we are searching together and stressed?"

He smiled a little at that. She wasn't wrong about the stress, but... How did he let her know this wasn't something he only wanted when they were searching?

"Maybe we let our guard down when we are searching."

"Or it slows us down long enough that we have time to think."

"Either of those would make sense. I don't want to scare you off..."

"Then don't."

"How are we supposed to have a relationship if we can't talk about things?" He met her eyes and tried to read whatever she was saying there, but Bre was better at hiding her emotions than she realized she was. She may feel like she made herself completely vulnerable, but she was excellent at downplaying or hiding her emotions. That was part of why it had taken Griffin so long before to allow her to know he had any kind of feelings for her.

Her eyes widened and there they were, flickers of something he couldn't identify, but saw that they were there.

"Is that what you want?"

He'd have to be the one to answer first, he knew, so Griffin took a breath and tried to find every ounce of his own courage. "Yes, it is. I'm not very good at relationships though."

"I'm worse."

"Sounds like a good match." He smiled at her, wondering if they were really going to do this.

A rustling in the leaves just then caught his attention and he held up a finger to his lips. Bre immediately stopped talking and both of them listened. Gauging her level of interest, Griffin looked at Ember. Her eyes were focused, her ears flicking back and forth, trying to pick up every sound in the air. He felt his breathing slow automatically as he prepared to face whoever was out there.

"Is it him again?" Bre whispered, and the tremor in her voice scared him because Bre wasn't scared of much. No one was fully invincible or unbreakable, and Bre was no exception. After having someone come after her over and over again, she had to be tired of feeling like the hunted.

He was tired of feeling like she was in constant danger.

Ember turned to him, eyes wide, and he told her to lie back down.

She did so, clearly unhappy with the command, but obeying anyway.

Griffin looked back at Bre, only to see that she'd scooted even further against the spruce tree, and had pulled out her weapon, which she was holding in the ready position. The good thing about that was that she no longer looked uncertain or afraid, just confident and ready to face whatever was out there.

They sat for Griffin wasn't sure how long, until Ember's ears settled back down and she laid her head on the ground, closed her eyes. If she was willing to nap, he wasn't worried anymore.

He looked behind him at Bre and saw that she'd already put her weapon away, apparently also watching his dogs for cues. Beside her, Flapjack had laid his head on her lap.

"I don't think we should try to sleep," she whispered to him as he came back under the tree. "It's not safe, clearly. I think he's still out there."

Any number of things could have made the noise they'd heard. This pass was teeming with wildlife large and small. Marmots, birds, bears, moose. He said as much to Bre, who shook her head. "It felt evil."

A shiver ran down Griffin's spine and he wished she wasn't right, but he knew what she meant exactly.

"I really want Addy to be okay." She brushed something from her cheek, probably a tear, Griffin figured.

"I do too."

Bre was shaking her head. "Why would she have come out here?"

The conversation shift was hard, but expected. They couldn't just sit out here and pretend like nothing was wrong. As much as Griffin would like to sit this close to Bre in the wilderness and just talk about a future between them, there were other things to focus on right now.

"Was this not a usual hiking spot for her?" He hadn't wanted to assume, though he could admit to feeling some frustration that Bre had allowed her niece to hike in a location known to be dangerous. Of course, that could describe all of Alaska, couldn't it? There might be a serial killer stalking this area, but he'd almost rather meet a serial killer than an adult black bear who had gone into stalker mode. Those tended to be even deadlier than grizzlies.

"She'd come out here before, but only with friends. She knew I discouraged it, though…" Bre's words trailed off. "Addy's a sweetheart, but like any teen I've ever met, she's got what we'll call an independent streak. I know at least once she made a comment about how I only didn't like it out here because of how badly that last search you and I worked together ended."

"Not a very nice comment."

Bre shrugged it off. "She's a kid. She was hurting, and it's been an adjustment for her to go from living with a single dad to her aunt, who is now functioning as a single mom."

"That makes sense."

"I managed to convince her eventually that it had more

to do with her safety and, as far as I know, she's only been out here a few times. Always with other people."

"And you're sure she didn't hike with anyone else the day she went missing?"

"Not that I know of. The police department hauled her car in, but I haven't heard anything yet. You don't think we get cell service here, do you? I could call in to them on my SAT phone..." She trailed off. "Of course, it might not be smart to use it, in case the killer is tracking us electronically somehow."

He hadn't considered that. "Do we need to turn our phones off?"

"I'm not going to." Bre shook her head. "I can't take the chance that Addy will try to get in touch with me and not be able to. That's more important to me."

"Let's check on the car tomorrow," Griffin suggested. "I may be able to use the dogs to get more information on whether other people were with her yesterday." The dogs processed information and then acted in the way they were trained to act, and Griffin, or whoever their handler was, had to interpret their behavior. Sometimes mistakes could be made, though usually they were made by the human handlers rather than by the dogs.

"Do you think knowing who she was with could help us find her? Would the hunter be after them both?"

It was hard to say.

"Maybe next time," he noted, "I'll tell my dogs to alert to any humans out here."

"I didn't know that was an option. That's probably not a bad idea."

Griffin agreed, especially since he hadn't considered the fact that Addy might have not come alone to the pass. What motivation would she have had for meeting someone or riding with someone out here that Bre wouldn't know about though?

They needed to search the car, but for that to happen, they had to make it out in the morning. He'd given up on managing to make it back to the car tonight.

He felt himself starting to nod off then looked over at Bre. She'd already fallen asleep. That was enough to wake him up. She was the one with the most expertise in situations like this, with a human element of danger, a "bad actor" as they'd refer to whoever was after them in the search-and-rescue world, and she felt like someone needed to keep watch.

She must be exhausted. He pulled the crinkly space blanket up at the edges so she was fully covered, and petted Flapjack's ears.

He'd take the first shift, then wake her and get some sleep later in the night.

As he sat there in the gathering dark, watching the woods, uncertainty started to gnaw at him. Would he be taking advantage of Bre's vulnerability if they started a relationship now? It seemed too good to be true that, after all these years, they'd be able to be together now. Was she right that it was stress from searching?

No, he knew the last wasn't true. What he felt for her was real. But did that make it right?

She looked so peaceful sleeping, he wanted that for her when she was awake too. Realistically, could he give her that? He was a man who second-guessed himself too often, who had once thought he had a place in the world and then had everything he'd thought he knew rearranged.

Almost everything. He still had his relationship

with God, something that, by Bre's own admission, she didn't have. Technically speaking, that should have been enough to motivate him to keep his lips to himself and refrain from taking their relationship to anything beyond friends.

He felt sick. He'd meant everything he'd said. He'd meant the kiss. He'd meant even more than he'd said aloud, because the truth was that he loved her.

But was love enough?

Griffin was afraid he didn't want to know the answer. More than that, he was afraid if he ever admitted the answer to himself, Bre would be hurt.

And that was exactly what he'd been trying to avoid.

THIRTEEN

When Bre opened her eyes, it took a minute for her to figure out where she was. Her chest was tight as she struggled to grasp why she was cold, who the dog with his head on her chest was. Somehow she'd fallen asleep, despite her determination to stay awake. But she was alive, and it was light outside. A new day. And unlike yesterday when they'd started the search, she had Griffin today, really on her side. Not just for the search, but maybe… Maybe in her life too?

Even though she'd stretched out on the ground and shouldn't have slept well, it had been some of the best rest she'd gotten in recent memory.

Bre pushed the space blanket down and sat up against the tree, doing her best to smooth out her hair, which was a mess. The fact that Griffin had seen her at her worst so many times and still seemed interested…

No, he'd seemed *more* than interested. She almost smiled just thinking about their kiss yesterday.

She worked on folding up the blanket, looking around for Griffin and Ember. She didn't see them anywhere and had just started to feel uneasy when he walked back into her vision from the left.

"Good morning. You sleep okay?" His smile was teasing.

"Like a rock. I'm sorry, I really did mean to keep an eye on things."

"I had it under control."

"You didn't have to do that."

"I wanted to."

That was something Bre almost couldn't understand. It was that strange to her to not have to carry things on her own.

"So, do you think we can head out now that we can see?"

"It's a risk. He knows we are going to want to make it back."

They were still at an enormous tactical disadvantage, something that irritated and scared Bre.

"Maybe we should just keep searching for now and head out later. That way, we aren't doing what he expects and, if he's waiting for us somewhere, he may give up."

He seemed to consider her idea. "Not a bad plan."

"Can the dogs search this many days in a row?"

"They'll be fine."

She reached down and petted Flapjack's head. He leaned into the attention.

"I'm almost awake enough to head out " She then paused to yawn. She was just moving toward Griffin. For a hug or a kiss, she hadn't decided yet, but he reached for her hand before she could make a move. She took it, still not believing this was really real.

"Bre, listen…"

Her heart crashed into her stomach. She heard it in his tone. Not knowing what had made him change his mind didn't diminish the fact that she could very clearly tell that he had.

"Let's just start walking back." She pulled her hand away. She didn't want to talk about it. Something about her repelled people; that was all there was to it.

She didn't know why she was surprised or hurt. Really, shouldn't she expect it?

Bre cares about someone. Person leaves Bre. It was normal. How. Life. Always. Worked.

One day she would stop expecting more and everything would be much easier.

"It's not you..."

"Don't, Griffin. I deserve better than that, don't you think?"

She didn't want to look up at him, because she knew his face, his eyes, would be more than she could steel herself against. After this search was over, she was going to have to never reach out to him again. Her heart simply couldn't handle getting this close and having her dreams dashed over and over. Everything had seemed so perfect last night. They matched; he understood her and seemed to still like her anyway.

Maybe he could have eventually even loved her? Not that Bre knew much about love. Everybody said it wasn't supposed to hurt, but she couldn't think of any time that it *hadn't*.

Her eyes stung and she brushed a tear from one of them before it could have the satisfaction of falling. She might not be able to stop them from leaking out, but she would *not* actively cry.

"That's the problem..." he started, "you deserve better than me."

She whirled around, hands on her hips. "That is ridiculous. Don't even start with me, Griffin. I don't want to hear it. If you don't want to be with me, say it. Don't be like this."

"I shouldn't have kissed you. You're vulnerable. You're hurting."

"I know my own mind. Unlike some people." She shoved the foil blanket into her backpack, slung it over her shoulders. "Are we going to search or not? I'd appreciate if we didn't waste any more time. The only family I have left is out here and I would like to get her back."

He stopped talking then, not that it eased the pain in her heart at all. Losing Griffin the first time had been hard enough, but with Ben's support and Addy's smiling face to show up now and then asking to watch silly made-for-TV movies at her house, when Bre knew full well that Addy hated those films, she'd made it through.

Without the two of them?

Bre couldn't think about it. This wasn't the time.

Flapjack stuck close to her side as she stood there, waiting for Griffin to finish packing up his bag. Finally, he was ready to go, too, and as he talked to both dogs, he snapped their vests on.

"I told them to search for anyone."

"Thanks. Good call."

They'd comb the pass and if no one else was out there, they'd go back to the Wolf River Police Department to see whether or not they could find anything in Addy's car. That had been a good idea.

Bre followed Griffin, letting her mind analyze their situation, make plans for later. No matter how she tried to spin it, she still needed Griffin's help if she was going to find her niece.

At what point did she give up? Not on Griffin, the

answer to that was pretty clear. He'd given up on her sometime in the middle of the night and just waited until she'd woken up to tell her. At least it had just been one kiss. She could almost write it off as a mistake and pretend she wasn't crushed, shrug it off, at least enough that he would think he hadn't hurt her as bad as he had.

But at what point did she give up on Addy...? This long after her disappearance, Bre was going to have to start to consider that question. The risk to both Bre and Griffin was high, and Bre knew from working with K-9 search teams before, that it was unusual that Griffin was willing to keep participating. He'd told her before, when they'd worked together years ago, that searchers always had the choice of whether or not they were willing to search and that, usually, if it was too high a risk to their own lives, they wouldn't. Sometimes kids kept them out longer or in more dangerous situations.

Obviously, the hunt for Addy was really why Griffin was staying out here, since it clearly had nothing to do with her.

She had to think about something else entirely. Her stomach was churning and Bre wished she had something else to eat, but they'd eaten the only snacks she'd had last night and she sure wasn't going to ask Griffin for anything, much as she already had to depend on him for the search when she didn't want anything from him.

Flapjack stopped walking then sprinted up ahead. Almost at the same moment that he kicked into gear, Ember did too.

"They've got something," she muttered to herself, proud of herself for recognizing it, but afraid to get her hopes up again.

Griffin had already picked up his pace and was hurrying after the dogs.

The K9s had run down a side trail, and Griffin followed, Bre close behind, thankful he wasn't trying to talk to her. Hope was trying to rise up inside her again, like maybe this would be the alert that found not just evidence of Addy being out here, but evidence that she was okay…

The dogs stopped and Griffin halted in front of Bre so quickly she almost ran into him.

"Stop, Bre—"

Bre kept walking. His voice didn't seem to hint at danger but rather…

Oh. *Oh.*

The dogs had laid down beside a beaten-down spot on the trail.

Even with the recent rain, Bre could see the blood on the plants. Not so much that she could say with certainty that her niece had died on this spot.

But enough that Addy surviving didn't have high odds.

A sob caught in her throat. She dropped to her knees and Flapjack broke his alert to come to her side. She wrapped her arms around the dog and cried, feeling like her heart was physically breaking. Her tears soaked his fur as she truly realized for the first time that she had failed. She'd let Ben down, lost the only family she had left. Once again, she had not been enough.

Spirit crushed, Bre admitted the truth to herself.

It was over. They had lost.

He had rewarded both dogs for their find, even though it wasn't the one he'd hoped for. But Griffin didn't say anything to Bre; he'd already done enough to hurt her.

He hadn't expected this particular alert today. Had actually prayed they wouldn't get it.

The dogs had smelled blood, though, which wasn't just like the smell of human remains, but similar enough.

"It might not be hers," he finally said to Bre as they started back to continue out of the pass.

"Don't give me false hope anymore, Griffin."

Her voice was empty.

He probably deserved her anger, but wished she understood he had never wanted to hurt her. When he'd told her he shouldn't have kissed her, that he didn't deserve her, he'd meant it. But maybe it had been the wrong thing to say. He believed in God and what God said, but so much of his life had been spent feeling like he didn't measure up. Maybe he was wrong.

Maybe it was his fault he had to live this halfway version of life where he didn't get the woman of his dreams and he lived alone forever.

He'd messed up again.

God, help me get her back. I know this is my third or fourth chance, but please...

The rest of the hike out of the pass was uneventful, the beautiful terrain looking just as vast and isolated as it always did, but with another extra bit of haunting danger today. Too much had gone wrong in this pass for Griffin to ever really see it like other people did. It would always be a place of heartbreak for him.

Mentally, he was struggling to pay attention to the dogs, though he was forcing himself to stay focused for Addy's sake. He wanted nothing more, besides finding her alive right now, than to be out of here. They needed something else. A plan. Or to investigate the car she'd driven to the pass. Something nagged at his gut about what Bre had said about Addy never hiking alone—yet she just happened to go alone one time and ended up a victim of foul play? That seemed too coincidental to be true.

After yesterday's hike and being shot at, this trek was almost too quiet. Griffin didn't know if it was because of the dogs' discovery of the blood—which Bre had gotten a sample of to send to the lab to confirm that it was Addy's, though his dogs' behavior left no doubt in his mind—or the way he'd mishandled the entire situation with him and Bre, but he was powerless to fix either. He could only be thankful that no one was shooting at them today. All of them, even the dogs, seemed to be moving slower than usual.

Once or twice, he glanced in Bre's direction and almost spoke, but there didn't seem to be a point. She was intentionally avoiding conversation with him, and he didn't blame her.

After the hope of yesterday, today felt even worse. And Griffin was fairly certain he couldn't fix any of it.

So instead, he continued to focus on the dogs but also on the pass around him, the noises that should be there, and willed himself to pick up any than shouldn't be. He might not be able to make Bre happy and give her the life he wished he could, but he could do everything in his power to help her stay alive.

Something that was clearly easier said than done with a killer lurking.

As soon as they'd reached the truck and started driving, Bre called the chief to update him on what had happened.

"But you're okay?"

"Yes." She knew he was talking about whether or not she was physically okay after the additional attacks. Emotionally, she was definitely not. She was still shaken, or something more than shaken, at feeling like she'd been so close to finally having something she'd dreamed about for so long, only to have it snatched away again. That applied to hope about Addy's possible survival and a relationship with Griffin.

Maybe it was time to admit that maybe people like her didn't fall in love, get married, have a family and a happily-ever-after. Maybe her childhood had made her fundamentally flawed in a way that she couldn't fix. Bre didn't know, but she was starting to think it was a dream she was going to have to let go of, at least with Griffin.

Who was the only man she'd ever felt strongly enough about to want a happily-ever-after with.

She brought her focus back to the case and the chief, and the questions she had. "Griffin was asking me about the car and it reminded me I hadn't heard from you. Have they finished processing it?"

"I believe so…" She heard the muffle of the receiver and him talking in the background. "Yes, they finished up last night, so, if you want to come take a look, you're welcome to."

"Thanks." She glanced over at Griffin, who was in at least as rough shape as she was. "I think we will clean up quick and then head over."

"Sounds good. We will see you then." She ended the call and looked over at Griffin. They hadn't spoken more than a handful of words to each other since earlier.

Was that really only this morning? It seemed to Bre that much more time had passed. They couldn't continue to work together without talking, though, and it seemed like it was up to her to address the awkwardness.

"The chief says we can look at the car. I'm assuming you don't mind coming with your dogs?"

"Of course not. Why would I quit in the middle of our investigation?"

Bre raised her eyebrow. It took Griffin a minute to look over since he was focused on driving, but he eventually did.

"Bre, I'm not quitting. On it, on you, on anything."

Sure looked like quitting to her, but the last thing she wanted to discuss was their personal...whatever it had been.

"I'm glad you're not quitting the search. I really need..." She'd almost said *you*, but that wouldn't be appropriate, now would it? It was definitely more than she cared to admit, and she was hoping it wasn't true in a general sense. "I really need your help. And the dogs, of course." She rubbed Flapjack's ears.

"I want to help." The way he said it felt final.

She just nodded once and said, "Good."

The drive to her house only took a few more minutes.

"Do you want to meet at the police station, or do you want to come back here after you clean up or whatever and we will ride together?" she asked.

"I'll meet you back here and we can go together. Don't leave the house or even go outside alone. I don't know how much experience you have with the arrows like the ones we saw, but they'll kill. Quickly. You might not have time to wait for help to arrive."

Besides, Bre thought, it turned out "help" might not be useful in the slightest. Not if a first responder really was involved, the way the FBI profilers thought. The idea made her squirm. Still, the idea of Griffin telling her what to do frustrated her.

"I don't plan to leave the house. I'll see you in a little while."

She thought he might have opened his mouth as she reached for the door handle, but when she looked back at him after she'd climbed out, he just shook his head and gave her a sad smile.

Followed closely by Flapjack, she went inside the house and locked the door behind her. She needed a shower, but she wasn't about to put herself in such a vulnerable position without double checking that the house was clear. Hand on her weapon, she moved through the house, clearing each room.

No evidence of anyone else's presence so far. Everything was as she'd left it.

When she got to Addy's room, she hesitated, hand on the knob. She'd only gone in here a handful of times since Addy had disappeared.

But today she wanted to be certain the entire house was empty. There was no one else to do it for her. Bre eased the door open, looked around the room that was so familiar. Addy's favorite colors, lavender and turquoise, were the theme. It was neat, but only to a point. Addy was too full of life and busy for every surface to be entirely clear of clutter.

She was proud of Addy. She might not be her mom, but she'd helped raise her niece in some ways, even before Ben had died. She'd taught her how to braid hair, handle bullies and make the best cupcake frosting. Being the aunt still meant they had a different sort of relationship, but in any event, Addy was her family.

Before she knew what she was doing, Bre walked

to the bed and sat on it, pulling one of Addy's pillows into her lap. As though sensing this was a private moment, Flapjack had stayed at the bedroom door and was just watching her.

The memory of the blood on the ground of the pass flooded Bre's mind and she felt her eyes burn and then a tear fall down her cheek.

She glanced at the bedside table, at the turquoise Bible sitting there. Hesitantly, she picked it up and opened it.

Addy's highlighting didn't make sense to her. Bre didn't know why certain sections of words would have had meaning, and her niece's notes in the margins weren't full sentences, but a word and a date, usually. It felt like an invasion of privacy to Bre, almost like reading someone's diary, but Addy wasn't there. And she felt that, if Addy knew what her mind was like right now…she'd want her to read.

Maybe Bre was curious. Addy would think there was still hope. Why? Was it because of this? She turned to the front, looking for some kind of topic index, but instead only found lists of books. She tried the back and there it was. Scanning down the page, she found the topic she wanted. Hope.

It took a few minutes for her to navigate the book and find the verses listed, but she read one after another. Her favorite was in the middle of the Bible, in a book called Psalms, chapter sixty-two, the fifth and sixth verses. *Yes, my soul, find rest in God; my hope comes from Him. Truly He is my rock and my salvation.*

She blew out a breath. Was it true? Addy would feel this way. Ben would have agreed with it. What allowed them to have hope when it didn't make sense though? The verses seemed to say it was God. But why?

She didn't know how to feel. She set the Bible down, but left it open in case she wanted to come back to read those verses again. Then she left the room, pulling the door behind her, more determined than ever to get her niece back. She had questions she wanted to ask her.

There were some things Bre might want to believe, if she understood how. But she needed someone to help her. And besides that, she missed her niece.

Please. She finally directed a prayer to God, heart pounding as she wondered if she was being foolish or if it would even work. *Please help me get her back, God. Don't let it be too late.*

FOURTEEN

"So if we know Addy was in the car, what good do the dogs do?" Bre asked an hour later as she and Griffin approached the police department. She'd had time to shower after her unexpected Bible browsing session, and then Griffin had returned and offered to drive, so she'd let him.

"I'm not sure." Bre appreciated his honesty. "I guess I just figured we may as well let them sniff, make sure they're connecting her scent... It was just an idea."

She wasn't sure why it was so important to her to look Addy's car over, either, other than the fact that she wondered if there might be any personal details evidence technicians might have overlooked as unimportant that could give her some kind of insight into what was happening.

"I think it's as good an idea as any. Just wondered," she said, to try to smooth things over, then just resigned herself to riding in silence. There had to be some way to make things less awkward between them, didn't there?

They parked in the WRPD lot and a wave of something like homesickness washed over Bre. She'd been relieved when the chief had told her she didn't need to come to work over the duration of the investigation, but at the same time, she missed it. The camaraderie, the atmosphere. These were her people.

Yet another reason the chief's revelation that the FBI thought a first responder was involved hurt her. Firefighters, EMTs—they were her people too. It made sense though. She still hadn't told Griffin what he'd said about that. She'd mention it to him tonight, in case he had any insights she didn't have on some of the responders who might be worth investigating further. It made her feel uneasy and uncomfortable to have to suspect people who devoted their lives to helping others, people who took risks to help other people.

Flapjack whined from where he had been left in the truck and Bre looked back at him.

"It's better to just have one for this. It's a small space—they'll just get in each other's way."

Ember was incredibly smart and focused. Griffin seemed to share a special bond with her, though, so Bre understood why, if he could only take one in, she would be the K-9 he would choose to work with.

Griffin opened the heavy glass front door and held it for her. Bre walked inside, drawing in a breath smelling of copy machine toner, old coffee and desk chairs from the 1990s.

The chief met them in the hallway. "The car's in the evidence bay." He led them there. Though it had only been a couple of days since Bre had been at work, she was fairly certain she hadn't forgotten her way around yet. But maybe this was part of being on leave; she wasn't technically working right now, so maybe that restricted her access.

The door to the evidence bay clanged open, echoing

in the large, garage-type room. Even though she knew they were there to see Addy's car, seeing it here, as *evidence*, was still a gut punch. A foolish part of her had continued to hope that Addy might have gotten lost or something equally benign in the pass, but every piece of evidence so far had disproved that theory.

That didn't make this any easier.

"We've got to keep it here for now, until we know exactly what we are dealing with," the chief stated. "But you're welcome to look through it. Bre, I need you to leave the contents for now…" He let his words trail off.

Bre nodded. Leaving Addy's personal items behind might be harder than she was anticipating, but it couldn't be any harder than being without Addy herself.

She opened the driver's-side door of the car, feeling more déjà vu than ever before. She'd done this plenty of times, including the day she'd bought this car with Addy in mind. She blinked, unwilling to let tears fall again.

This was going to be harder than she'd thought. Still blinking, she moved back, motioning to Griffin. "Want to let Ember sniff?"

He was holding out one of the socks that she'd given him to use as scent markers. Ember was wearing her vest—he must have put it on the dog when Bre'd been overwhelmed looking at the car—and now the dog looked focused.

As Bre stood back and watched, Ember leapt into the car, her red fur striking and almost regal as she performed her job. She sniffed around inside, pausing now and then, and then she sat in the passenger seat, barked, and looked straight at Griffin.

When Bre glanced over at him, he was frowning.

"What?" she asked. "What is it?"

He shook his head, moved to the other side of the car and eased open the passenger door. He gave Ember what looked like a piece of hot dog, then called her down out of the car. Griffin took the vest off her, squatted and petted her, murmuring in a low voice.

Bre didn't know if this was something that was normal for a search, or what, but it wasn't making sense to her.

The chef stood off to the side, eyebrows raised.

She didn't know what she thought yet. Police officers were used to building strong cases in court and she knew that anyone having a "feeling" about something would not hold up as evidence. It was difficult to accept the fact that the K-9 wasn't having a feeling, that she had smelled something, an intangible something, but actual evidence nonetheless. But this was different from their search with the dogs in the woods.

Ember had alerted, or at least Bre thought so. But why in the passenger seat?

Bre watched as Griffin put the vest back on and asked her to search again, this time starting her in the back of the vehicle, with the lift gate open. Ember jumped up, sniffed around the cargo area, where Bre tried not to notice the running shoes in the corner. She hadn't expected seeing Addy's possessions to hit her this hard. They were only things; they weren't the person missing, but they were a physical reminder. A gut punch that reminded her that her niece was gone.

Bre saw herself cleaning out this car. Packing Addy's room. Was that her future? Was that how this would all end?

Shaken, she tried to focus on Ember. The dog moved

around the car, sniffing, then went back to the front passenger seat, sat, barked, then looked at Griffin.

This time, Bre walked over to him as he motioned Ember to heel. "What's going on?"

"Addy wasn't the last person to drive the car."

Of all the things he could have said, that was one of the least expected. As far as they knew, Addy had been alone the day she went missing. "What?" Even when they'd wondered whether or not she could have driven with someone, no one had ever considered that Addy might not have been the one driving her own car. Suddenly it seemed like a huge blessing that Griffin had wanted Ember to search the car.

The chief moved closer. "What's going on?"

"Sir, I don't believe Addy was the one who drove her car last. Scent pools in places where people spend time. The entire car smells like Addy. I can tell that from Ember's behavior, and just plan logic. But I would expect her scent to have pooled in the driver's seat, since this is her car. But it is pooled in the passenger seat."

"Which means…?"

Griffin just looked at Bre. "I'm the dog handler. I interpret the information I get. You're the police officers."

It seemed to be the encouragement her mind needed to fill in the blanks and come up with ideas, possible explanations.

"It means Addy wasn't driving…" she began, "which means…" She blew out a breath. "Addy wasn't allowed to let her friends drive her car. So either she broke that rule—"

"Or she didn't have a choice," the chief interjected. "Or it was an adult and she thought the rule might not apply."

"Why would she believe an adult needed to drive her car though?"

Bre was now having no trouble coming up with ideas. "An adult could have said any number of things to convince a teenager. Maybe if they said something happened to me and offered to drive in case she was too upset after hearing about my supposed injury or death. Maybe they just asked if she minded if they drove and it because it was an adult asking, she said yes. Or someone held her at gunpoint and didn't give her a choice."

"No signs of a struggle, though," the Chief pointed out.

"True…" Bre trailed off. "So back to the first two options."

"Either way, it changes the entire way we look at this," the chief said in a tight voice.

"That she wasn't driving?" Griffin asked.

Bre closed her eyes and blew out a breath. "No. That's not it. It's the fact that in any scenario where the adult drove…the adult was someone she knew."

The ride from the police department back to Bre's house was even quieter than the ride there had been.

Until Bre finally broke the silence.

"The FBI profilers think the serial killer is a first responder."

She spoken simply, though the impact of her words was like an explosion to him.

In the aftermath, he sat blinking, driving but only sort of seeing what was in front of him. Finally, he gave up and pulled over.

"What are you doing?" she asked, her voice strained.

"I need a second, okay? How long have you known that's what the profilers said?" He looked over at her.

She wouldn't meet his eyes.

"Hours?" he asked, but Bre still didn't answer.

"Days?"

She nodded.

He'd thought they were a team, that he had been helping her. In the beginning it had felt like they were actually working together, fully, bouncing ideas off of each other. She'd kept him entirely in the dark about something it would have been important for him to know.

"Only a couple of days. I just didn't know how to tell you. It hit me hard and I knew it would hit you hard too."

"You didn't just want to keep it from me?"

He looked over at her as he asked and her brows pressed together, her face anguished. "Why would you think I would intentionally keep it from you?"

It was a valid question. He felt like she was pulling away from him in every way possible—not that he could blame her—but that didn't mean she would intentionally withhold information that could help in the investigation they were working together. He felt his frustration ease.

"I'm sorry… I just… A first responder?"

She nodded. He blew out a breath and eased the truck back onto the road.

"We need to make a list of everyone who is a first responder and could be a suspect. I started a list the other day when you were searching in the pass without me, but I'd like your help going over it. I'm sure the Chief probably has someone doing the same, but sine I'm not part of the official case anymore, I don't have access to it."

"That would be a long list. You know how it is here, with emergencies. That would encompass all the first responders in our town, in the surrounding towns…" Bre paused as a thought hit her. "Except, if Addy knew them, it narrows it down."

"Do you feel like you know every possible first responder she would have known?"

"I think so." She didn't sound certain, though, and Griffin hoped she was right. The atmosphere in the truck had changed. It felt like the air does right before a rainstorm, heavy with expectation, about to burst, but not quite. First, the waiting.

The waiting was always the worst.

They pulled into Bre's driveway, and she wasted no time hurrying inside. Griffin was left to follow behind her. She was like a whirlwind now that she had somewhere to look, something to focus on.

Inside Bre's house, Griffin, Ember and Flapjack watched as she transformed her small kitchen eating nook into something like a war room. First, she cleared the table, which Griffin helped with, carrying crossword puzzle books and a few empty coffee cups to the kitchen counter and sink.

"I need all the news articles for this case so far. I could print them off…"

"Got it." Griffin had his phone out before she was even done talking, looking at the local news site and sending them to Bre's printer.

"Okay, and sticky notes…"

"Point me in the right direction."

"Top drawer by the dishwasher." She pulled out a chair and sat.

Griffin dug through the drawer and found not just

sticky notes but a notebook and several pens. It was the most organized junk drawer he'd ever seen, if he could even call it that.

"I need to know everyone who has been part of the case." She started writing and he saw in her face the desperation. They weren't going to solve this in a night.

Right?

The doorbell rang. Griffin hurried to answer it, leaving Bre to brainstorm. He found the chief and another officer.

"I don't feel good about Bre being here alone, after all the continued attacks. I managed to get approval to have an officer stationed here during the rest of the time the case is open."

Griffin heard Bre's footsteps behind him. "Thanks, Chief."

It said a lot to Griffin that she didn't argue with him about the extra security around her house.

The older man nodded once. "We will head out now, but I wanted to let you know so you didn't wonder why he was outside."

"Thanks." Bre smiled, but she was clearly distracted. Griffin knew she wanted to get back to work.

As soon as the door was shut, she turned to him. "You may as well head home if you want to get some sleep or have things to do. I have security outside, so I shouldn't have the same issues as the other night." She offered a small smile and Griffin couldn't tell if she was looking out for him or if she wanted to get rid of him. Possibly both.

"I'd rather help you brainstorm," he told her, watching her expression. "But maybe I could go pick up some lunch for us?"

Her stomach growled as if on cue and Griffin laughed. "I'll leave Ember with you and Flapjack if that's okay? She's likely to eat the food if she comes with me in the truck."

"But she's so well behaved."

"It doesn't always extend to food."

"Same, though." Bre laughed and, for a second, Griffin felt as though things were like they were before. Before this morning. Before last night's kiss—that shouldn't have happened. Just the easygoing friendship they'd had for so many years.

Why had he messed that up?

He swallowed hard against the familiar feeling of failure that threatened to submerge him. "Any food preferences?"

"Not burgers."

"Got it."

Making sure he waited until he heard the click of the door locking behind him, Griffin walked to his truck.

The Chinese food truck in Wolf River was one of the best restaurants he'd ever ordered from. Once he arrived, he ordered his favorite and a couple things he thought he remembered Bre liking. It seemed like so long ago, but once he started ordering he remembered that, years ago, he, Ben, Bre and a much younger Addy would share Chinese food on Friday nights. Maybe that was why this had been his first thought for something different to eat.

The fact was, he realized as he waited for the food, Bre's past was so entangled with his that it was hard to isolate her impact on his life to just one area. They'd been through a lot together, and a lot more apart. He should have been there for Bre after Ben's death, and he wanted to make it up to her. At the moment, he was doing a pretty terrible job of it so far. And then there was that kiss. The last thing he'd intended to do was to take advantage of her grief and kiss her the other day. Did she know that? What did she think of him?

He had to stop thinking about that night and all the things he'd done wrong. The dogs would pick up on his insecurity and not feel as confident when they were searching. Even though they'd paused the search for now, unsure where to look next after the discovery of the blood on the pass and the scent pool Ember had alerted to in Addy's car, they could end up needing Ember and Flapjack to search again. He had to project some confidence.

Griffin would just have to work on finding some.

He picked up the food when it was ready and made the drive back to Bre's house.

When he walked in, the amount of work she'd done in only about an hour amazed him. The windows in her breakfast nook were covered in a colorful chaos of sticky notes, words and phrases scrawled on each. There was a piece of poster board—she had poster board in her house somewhere?—taped to the window, a list of names on it. Possible suspects, he was guessing. He flinched at some of the names included. It was hard to believe that anyone they knew personally would be capable of the kind of atrocities the Echo Pass Hunter had previously committed, much less also be responsible for Addy's disappearance.

"You've been busy," he said as he set the Chinese food on the counter.

"You're back! It's been that long?" She looked up at him, slightly dazed, and Griffin smiled at her.

"You're doing an amazing job." He held out his arms, not sure whether she'd accept the hug for the offer of friendship that it was. Something flickered on her face, but she walked into his arms and he folded her into a hug.

He could stay like this forever, just keeping her safe, feeling like he wasn't failing at life. Except, they couldn't actually, because there were things to do.

"I need another set of eyes on this," she said, looking up at him.

"Let's eat first."

She hesitated.

"Five minutes. You need to eat a little. Did you remember to eat this morning?" They hadn't had much when they'd been lost in the woods yesterday and, with all the stress, she needed to keep her energy up. Griffin wasn't surprised, though, when she shook her head, but he persisted. "Eat first. Then we'll see what we can figure out."

To his surprise, she didn't argue.

He fixed them both plates, though Griffin found he wasn't very hungry. Thinking of Addy out there alone had stolen some of his appetite. His stomach twisted in nervous anticipation. He hadn't felt quite like this yesterday. Was it thinking of the blood on the ground of the pass?

Or did he sense somehow that Bre was about to break the case wide open?

FIFTEEN

Bre couldn't believe how much better food made her feel. For the first time in days, she had extra energy and had the desire to push herself to find Addy. Urgency seemed to press at her.

"Do you think God ever tells people things, like the future?" she asked Griffin, hating how weird the question sounded to her ears but not sure how else to phrase it.

"What do you mean?"

She shook her head. "I don't know. I just…" She struggled to find the words, tried to find a way to describe to him the pressing against her chest, the anticipation fluttering in her stomach. "I don't feel anxious about Addy, not any more than usual, I mean. I'm scared for her—I have been this whole time. But today I just feel like I *have* to find her."

"I have too," Griffin said, his voice honest.

"So does God do that?"

He seemed to be searching her eyes for something, maybe because of the way she'd reacted the last time he had tried to bring up God. Now here she was willingly discussing Him. But she didn't have time to tell him about sitting in Addy's room with the Bible and wondering if there was something to it. Since she'd looked up those verses, it did feel like maybe God was real? And could potentially care about her and her family? All Bre knew for sure was that she didn't feel as alone as she had before she'd read those verses.

Now she felt like she was supposed to hurry. No more wasting time.

"Maybe," Griffin finally said. "I don't know exactly how God works. None of us does. I will tell you that God can speak to us however He wants. He could very well be making you feel a certain way."

"So that I hurry up and find her in case she's still alive?" Impractical as she knew she was being at this point, Bre still couldn't quite bring herself to really consider the alternative. She desperately wanted and needed Addy to be okay.

"God is in control. You aren't the one in control of the outcome here."

Blinking, she nodded her head, but that was all she could handle for now. She was too overwhelmed with emotions to speak.

She turned away from Griffin and motioned to the window, taking a breath before speaking. "So, here's what I got while you were gone."

"You did a lot."

"I had a lot of thoughts. I made a list of all the people I know of who are working this case. Lots of police, a couple firefighters who came to help with the search, some locals who I know helped search at some point. You're the only search-and-rescue worker that I know of, at least with a dog. There could have been more at the initial search. I would need to ask the chief who all showed up, or if any kind of log was kept, the day that I spent in the pass searching—the first day she was missing." She reached down and petted Flapjack, who hadn't strayed far from her the entire day. He seemed to sense her unease with whatever this feeling was she was wrestling with.

"I don't know of any other search dog teams who have been out." Griffin stepped closer. "So, on this map of the pass—" he motioned to the map she'd hung in one of her windows "—the red X marks are...?"

"Where the Echo Pass Hunter's victims have been found."

She watched as he studied the map, tracing his finger around it, from one red X to the other. "This one is Megan and the avalanche, right?"

"Yes."

"And this one?"

"A case a couple of years ago. Missing woman in her late thirties. Someone visiting from the Lower 48 who disappeared on a hike."

"Near where the main trail splits off and the Wilderness Rim ridgeline hike is?"

"Yep."

He was frowning now. "I worked a case there years ago when I was still with the SAR team. Missing toddler. We found him—he'd gotten lost when on a hike with his family."

"It's an easy area to get lost in."

Griffin went back to staring at the map. She appreciated his attention to detail, but at the same time, she wanted to focus on something new. Didn't see any kind of pattern that would show them where to look for Addy. Sometimes the killer left his bodies by water; sometimes he buried them in a shallow grave under a spruce tree. Sometimes the body was found in the middle of a hiking trail. There didn't seem to be any connection in deposit sites.

"Bre." His tone was firm, his brow slightly creased. "And this one?"

"It's hard to explain." That recovery had been one she had been a part of, due to her size. The department had needed someone light to repel in to retrieve the body from a small cliff ledge. There'd been no blood at the scene, so the body had been moved posthumously. They assumed the killer had tried to dispose of the remains over the side of the cliff, and then missed and accidentally dropped it straight onto the ledge.

"On a ledge, right? About fifteen, twenty, feet down a cliff?"

Now it was Bre's turn to frown. "I don't understand."

"I should have seen…" He moved to the articles he'd printed for Bre earlier about Addy's disappearance. She hadn't had a chance to look through those yet. He looked up at Bre.

"All of the places you marked on the map are where a body was found? I've worked searches and found a victim at all of those locations."

"Someone is trying to set you up somehow?" she asked, but he was shaking his head.

"No. I don't see any reason to think that. But I think it's someone I worked with. Someone who had been to these sites."

Her eyes widened. "Joseph."

How she hadn't seen it before, Bre didn't know either. Probably because it wasn't normal to identify people she knew as potential serial killers, she reminded herself before she could beat herself up too badly. She didn't know him well, but it was still strange. And if they were right and he was their prime suspect, then the FBI would be right, too; he was a first responder.

It made sense though. He hadn't been with them the day that the avalanche had killed Megan. He'd been sick, he'd said. Too much exposure to the cold during the search for Megan the day before, he'd said. Bre had never felt entirely comfortable around him, but she'd chalked it up to her own insecurity, since she didn't understand the nuances of canine SAR work the way he and Griffin did.

Now Bre wondered if that was indeed the reason. Or if he'd been her killer.

He was the only one she knew of who had almost always searched with Griffin, had been with him at all of those locations.

It fit.

"So Addy should be…"

"Somewhere that has meaning to him. Likely somewhere he's worked a search before."

She was already scrambling for another map, she'd printed several copies off, and some highlighters and Sharpies. When in doubt, her past had taught her to be organized. Make lists. It didn't usually help but it sure made her feel better.

Except this time it might help. If they could figure out where Addy was, they could find her.

"All of these women were dead when we arrived though." Bre looked up at Griffin, shaking her head.

"It's the best lead we have. Get the maps. Call the chief and tell him what we think and that we're going back into the pass."

Bre grabbed all the supplies they would need and shoved them into a bag. Both dogs were running in circles at their feet now.

"Ready to go find her?" She bent to ask Ember and Flapjack.

Their bright, eager eyes seemed to say yes. They were so full of hope. *Hope.* The verses Bre had read earlier came back to her mind somehow, even though she'd only read them over a few times. *Yes, my soul, find rest in God; my hope comes from Him. Truly he is my rock and my salvation.*

Thanks, God.

They hurried to the truck and Griffin turned them in the direction of the pass.

"While you drive, tell me all the places you remember working searches."

As they rumbled up the mountain road to the isolated parking lot, she made notes on the maps, marked possible locations.

They were going to find her. Bre could feel it.

Her stomach churned. If only Bre was sure this was a good thing. But the sense of uncertainty and urgency she'd had earlier hadn't left. It had magnified instead and brought with it a heavy blanket of dread.

Hope. Dread.

She didn't know which would win, but they were fighting over her right now.

God, help. If we're wrong about Joseph, show us who is behind this. And if we are right, help us figure out where he has Addy.

Bre had called the chief to let him know they were going to search the pass again, and to tell him who they thought the Hunter might be. He'd promised to investigate Joseph more thoroughly on his end.

"And, Bre?" Griffin had heard him say. "Be careful."

Griffin was fairly certain a standard background check wouldn't turn up anything, but when he said so to Bre she'd said there were still plenty of things for the Chief to find. Odd inconsistencies in stories he told friends and neighbors, timelines of where he'd been and when that could place him at the pass when women had been abducted. There were lots of avenues to investigate.

Ember seemed to sense the intensity of Bre's emotions and looked ready to get to work. Flapjack, too, looked more serious than Griffin was used to seeing him. He'd been amazed over the last couple of days at how he'd attached to Bre though. When this was over, he was probably going to have to see if she wanted to make the arrangement permanent. He had the feeling his dog's heart had been as completely stolen by Bre as his own had.

The differences, he berated himself, was that the dog knew better than to mess everything up. He, apparently, didn't.

But, he reminded himself, he hadn't wanted to. Part of it had been him second-guessing himself, sure, but part of the reason for stopping things with Bre from going any further had been the fact that faith was something too big to disagree with a spouse about. He'd known couples who had tried to ignore their conflicting beliefs and it had come back to bite them. Bre's hostility toward any mention of God the other day had caused him to back off too.

It had been a lot of things. He loved her. But it never seemed to be the right time. Maybe he was destined to be alone. Griffin knew with certainty that if he couldn't be with Bre, solitude would be his preference. No one had ever held a candle to her. It had been part of the reason he and Megan had broken up, in fact. She'd recognized that his heart had belonged to someone else and there hadn't been room for anyone else in it.

There was an extra sense of urgency as they parked and unloaded the gear this time. Griffin went through the motions of readying the dogs for the search, giving them the scent, and putting their harnesses on.

"You have the maps?" he asked Bre.

She nodded. "One here." She lifted it up, along with a Sharpie. "And extras in my backpack."

"Good."

They started walking.

"Griffin," Bre said as they made their way through the alders that marked the first mile or so of the trail that gently started leading upward into the mountain pass, "you've worked a lot of cases, right?"

"Yeah."

"How many in this pass?" It was hard to put a number on it, and the look on his face must have said so, because Bre made a face at what she apparently considered long odds. "That's what I figured."

"We're going to find her," he said.

She nodded. "I hope so. I think we really might."

"Let's go up the ridgeline again. That's one place the dogs alerted the other day that I think we could stand to investigate further. The problem is, we don't know when she was where, only that the dogs alerted in multiple areas of the pass."

"Okay. Did you have searches in that direction that Joseph worked with you?" Her hands were shaking, Griffin noticed, but from anticipation or anger, he wasn't sure.

"I think so. Most of us worked together for all the searches."

The brush thickened as they walked deeper into the alders, and Griffin found himself tensing. This was one of the areas that always made him uneasy. For increased bear activity, if nothing else. Bears loved alders, and the thickness of the low trees here on the pass made it ideal for bear habitat. The serial killer wasn't the only danger they faced in these Alaskan woods.

As they climbed toward the ridgeline, Griffin searched his brain for cases that stood out. Serial killers had strange habits, which explained why the Echo Pass Hunter, if it was Joseph, would have chosen locations where their search-and-rescue team had recovered bodies before. Those were areas of significance to him. Why he'd started killing, or if it had anything to do with his searches, was anyone's guess. Too often with serial killers, it seemed, from what little he knew of them, there were questions left unanswered.

"The cabin," he said to Bre then they were on top of the ridge. "I bet he's got her at the cabin."

"Did you recover anyone there?"

Griffin was already nodding. "A man in his twenties who had fallen while climbing with friends. He'd gotten disoriented and wandered off, and when he recovered, he couldn't find his friends. He managed to find a cluster of old cabins and sheltered there for days... Joseph commented then that people could hole up there and no one would ever know. They were part of the park system once, but they fell into disrepair and sort of fell off the books…"

"Which way?" Her voice was urgent. He'd apparently convinced her.

He motioned up the trail and then pointed to the side of the mountain ahead of them. They'd need to traverse the ridgeline, being extra cautious with the dogs not to lose their footing or risk anyone's safety.

Ember alerted again and Griffin hurried to her and examined the ground. Dark brown droplets that were not plant material underfoot confirmed that she'd alerted to blood again.

"More blood?" Bre's eyes were full of fear.

"Hey, we won't know anything until we find her, okay?"

"But she came this way."

He nodded.

"So you think he brought her back to his cabin or…?"

"It's impossible to guess."

"You're right." Her voice betrayed her frustration. "I just want to know."

The pass opened up as they scaled the side of the mountain now, traversing a trail cut into the cliff's edge. Griffin remembered the severity of the injuries of the climber who'd fallen. That was something he wanted both of them to avoid. Especially since no one knew exactly where they were.

"Careful," he urged her. "You didn't tell the chief where we were going specifically, besides the pass, did you?"

"How could I? I didn't know till just now, remember?"

She was right. There was no way, but Griffin wished now that they had backup.

"He was at the search," Bre said to him absently, as though she'd just remembered. "I saw him that first day. He looked a little surprised to see me. Like maybe he didn't know that Addy was my niece? But he recognized me."

"And now he's been after you."

She nodded.

"Probably because he realized he'd made a mistake in who he went after this time. It's one thing to kill or abduct someone's family member and to have them want to bring you to justice, but they don't have the skills. This time he messed with someone who has the talent needed to put him away for life and end all of this."

"No pressure," she said, voice tight.

"You've got this, Bre. You've been amazing this whole time."

A short, humorless laugh. "So amazing you couldn't wait to push me away again, huh?"

"Push you away? Is that what you think—"

"I shouldn't have said anything." Either it was his imagination, or she'd picked up the pace, but she was behaving as if she could outrun this awkwardness between them if she just hiked a little faster. "We can talk about it when this is over. If we find Addy."

"*When* we find Addy."

Nothing else was said as the terrain became more technical. The dogs handled it like champs, but several times Griffin had to use his hands to steady himself and continue climbing up. These cabins had been fairly inaccessible, part of the reason the state had stopped maintaining them. As he remembered it, the building he was looking for had been an old trapper's or miner's cabin, he couldn't remember which, from days when Alaska was even more wild and untamed.

"There it is." He stopped and pointed. Immediately both dogs alerted.

The cabin was up ahead, exposed, with no way to approach that wouldn't let the occupants know someone was there.

Of course, they'd been shot at by arrows enough times now, he shouldn't be dreading the approach this much. But maybe that made it worse. Even if the man had missed multiple times, he was likely to hit Bre eventually. And, like he'd told her, with the arrows he was using, there might not be a chance to save her, not if it hit her in the wrong place.

"Griffin, I'm scared," she finally whispered. "What if…?"

"Hang on to some hope, okay?" He grabbed her hand and squeezed, then let it go. And said a quick prayer that he wasn't giving her false hope. Or walking them both into some kind of trap.

He couldn't count all the dangers up here on one hand. The fine edge between life and death seemed even thinner up here, in the isolated backcountry. Life was precious, Griffin believed that, but right now Bre's was at risk. His too.

And Addy's, if she was still alive.

Addy's life made their risks worth it.

Please, God, please.

Griffin took a deep breath and reached for Bre's hand one more time. They started toward the cabin, half afraid of what they would find.

SIXTEEN

They hadn't gotten shot on their way to the cabin, which seemed to bode well. Maybe the killer wasn't there but had left Addy behind, if Griffin's guess was right. If that was the case, though, Addy would be in rough shape, if she were alive at all. Possibly too far gone to save.

Admitting that felt like giving up, though, and Bre wasn't going to do that. Not yet, when they might be so close.

Please let her be here. She found herself asking God, trying hard to believe He might be listening. Her childhood faith was seeming closer and closer, almost within her grasp. She didn't understand though.

Do you really want a God you can understand? The words echoed in her mind. Addy had asked her the same thing once. Bre hadn't known the answer then and wasn't sure she knew it now either. Part of her thought yes. But what kind of God was that, if He wasn't any bigger or more complicated than she was?

Griffin reached for the front door of the cabin and turned to her. "Ready?" he asked, but she didn't know the answer to that either.

Her mind seemed to have emptied itself of every

thought except *Find Addy*, which seemed to thump in her chest along with her heartbeat. *Find Addy. Find Addy.* As Griffin eased the door open, she tried to steel herself for whatever she might see. The heavy cabin door creaked only slightly on its hinges.

"Let me go first, in case he's in here, or in case…" Griffin didn't finish, but Bre knew what he meant. She let him go in first, then followed, easing the door shut with a quiet thud behind her. Her eyes weren't adjusted to the dim light. The cabin had windows—she had seen them from the outside—but some kind of fabric obscured them, cutting the room off from the light. The air was thick, stale, and nothing like the fresh air they'd just been breathing outside.

Much as she didn't want to, the law enforcement side of her noticed immediately that there was no smell of bodily decomposition. While that was good news, she didn't even want to be thinking of her precious niece and corpses in the same sentences. But the fact that there was no cloyingly awful stench of death was a good sign.

A thin layer of dust coated everything in the cabin, from the small coatrack by the door to the old bed in the corner, covered by wool blankets. It was disturbed in places, like someone could have been there lately, but the bedding had not been cleaned in ages. On one wall there was a fireplace, another wall had shelves lined with all kinds of essentials. From where she stood just inside the door, Bre could see normal household supplies: a couple of metal camping-style plates, duct tape, tools, extra blankets. Whether someone like the Echo Pass Hunter was living there or people just kept it stocked for when others stayed, she wasn't sure.

Caution slowing her steps, Bre moved further inside the room, and took her time examining the corners for anywhere a person could hide. She couldn't take the chance that Addy could be there, and they could miss her, if she was paralyzed with panic and unable to let them know she was there. She looked in every corner, under the small shelves, in the corner where a curtain was hanging below a shelf, making a sort of makeshift cabinet.

But no Addy.

The bed was empty. No one was under it.

No one was in the cabin.

Nor was there any visible evidence that she had been there. The dogs weren't even alerting now, though they had alerted outside the cabin when they'd first approached. Bre had been so sure…

"She's not here," Griffin said, stating what had become obvious to both of them.

"She's not," Bre agreed, swallowing hard against her disappointment. "So…"

"So we go outside and keep hiking." His voice was full of conviction and determination. He never gave up, Griffin. It was something else she liked about him.

Bre looked over at him and, in the dingy cabin, finally admitted the full truth to herself.

His determination was one of the things she *loved* about him. Through this entire ordeal he had been steadfast, encouraging, and always willing to help however he could. These were the qualities of a man worth loving, whether or not he believed in himself, and Bre did. Even if nothing happened between them, and it was fairly clear at this point that nothing ever would, she was ready to admit that was how she felt.

"We've been looking for so long."

"It doesn't matter how long it takes. I'm not giving up."

She met his gaze then and could have vowed she'd seen something that hinted he wasn't only talking about the search for her niece. Bre didn't know what to say, so she just nodded. Her heart was exhausted from the feeling of having her hopes so high only to come crashing down again, and her body was exhausted from the hike up here. Her arm ached.

She didn't want to give up either. Definitely not on Addy.

But she didn't want to give up on Griffin either. He'd hurt her, but she'd been acting this entire time like she was the only one with hurts, with regrets and fears that chased at her. He was also only human, and this entire time she'd been behaving as though Griffin should somehow be superhuman, not needing any of her affirmation. As if he was the only one who'd made mistakes and needed encouragement to move forward, start anew.

Maybe it was time she made sure that he knew she wasn't giving up on him. Not this minute when they were in an old cabin on the side of a mountain. But soon.

Instead, for now, she offered him a small smile. "Let's go keep searching then."

He eased the door open and she followed him into the sunshine. She inhaled deeply, her lungs filling with fresh air. It didn't take long for Ember to catch Addy's scent again, and they were following her behind the cabin when the first whoosh split the air.

"Get *down*!" Griffin yelled with more force than she'd ever heard him use. But before she could do what he'd said, sudden agony bloomed in her shoulder—the same one where she'd been hit previously. She glanced down, her eyes blurring with tears at the pain, and saw another arrow sprouting from her body. The force was great enough that she fell to the ground, crying out in shocked agony.

Griffin turned to her, but Bre could see the silhouette of the killer beyond him, close enough that he wouldn't know, bowstring drawn back. His identity was concealed by the glaring sunlight, but she didn't need to know it was Joseph for sure to know that Griffin was in danger.

"Griffin, no!"

As she yelled, Flapjack ran to her and she did her best to pull him into her arms to keep him safe, knowing that someone who could kill as many people as the Echo Pass Hunter likely had wouldn't hesitate to hurt a dog.

Ember barked and growled, a much more intimidating sound than Bre would have predicted the dog able to make. Digging her paws into the ground to run as fast as she could, the K-9 charged the man with the bow, who adjusted his aim to target her. But he missed, to thrown off balance by Ember's sudden movement to hit anyone.

Griffin tackled the man and fought to disarm him. Both were evenly matched and Bre watched, doing her best to ignore the searing pain in her shoulder. Her shirt was sticking to her wound and she could smell blood. No telling how much she was losing. The hunter—she could see his face now—was Joseph. He was on top, his hands going around Griffin's throat. Ember was beside them, growling, barking, attempting to bite at the man's leg. Flapjack was beside her, growling low and threatening.

Finally, Joseph turned his attention to the dogs, which

seemed to be all the motivation Griffin needed to find a little more strength to deck the man in the jaw. Bre heard the pop and saw the killer go down on the ground. Still.

Then it was quiet. Was the Echo Pass Hunter dead? Was Addy? Was Griffin? She needed to find out, but her arm was hurting badly enough now that she was getting dizzy. She had to call this in, get help, and not just for her but in case Griffin was hurt...

And Joseph as well. After all, she wanted to see him *pay* for his crimes by standing trial, not just get away with them by dying before he was held accountable for the the evil he had done.

She felt in her pockets for her phone, in case by some chance she got service. Alaska had the strangest coverage, and they were high up, so it wasn't out of the question.

Please God, I could use a break here.

Two bars. Enough.

She called the police department and spoke to the chief. Before they disconnected, he promised to send men by helicopter as soon as he could get one of the emergency choppers the town used to medivac people to Anchorage.

Then she tried to crawl toward Griffin and stopped. Her arm made it impossible to move, the pain was that bad. Bre squeezed her eyes shut. Finally, she managed to edge her way closer, a couple of feet at a time.

Griffin was sitting up, out of breath, but apparently fine. Ember looked good, as well, unscathed even after her fight.

"You're such a good girl" Bre said with a smile. She looked up to check on Flapjack and saw that her words had brought him to her side already. She petted him and assured him he was a good boy as well, relieved to find that he didn't appear to have any injuries also.

"Griffin, can you catch?" she called over to him as she winced and used her good arm to pull her handcuffs out of her back pocket. She'd brought them along tonight hoping against hope they would be able to get to use them.

And You made it happen. God, thank You, Bre told God.

It seemed like He had been more involved than Bre had given Him credit for.

She tossed the handcuffs to Griffin, heard the clank of the metal as he caught and secured them around the still unconscious man's hands. He'd just latched them shut when Joseph started to rouse.

Now she felt like she didn't have a choice but to push through. Police were on their way and this was her only chance to talk to Joseph, to look him in the face and ask why he'd done it. And where Addy was.

The pain was suffocating but she made it, barely, after pushing up to her feet with her good hand and walking slowly to where the men were.

"So it was you," she said as she saw Joseph clearly, lying on the ground, regaining consciousness. His medium brown hair was messy, his skin pale. Strange to see someone who had wreaked so much havoc, stolen people's lives, in a position of such vulnerability. Some part of her wanted to kill him where he lay, repay him for the evil he had done. But she knew that wasn't the way to handle it, wasn't what the law or God demanded.

It wouldn't bring back anyone he'd killed.

It would not bring back Addy.

Bre took a deep breath. Any minute, her chance

would be over. She had questions she had to ask, answers that she had to know. She only prayed she was strong enough to handle them.

"Why?"

Bre's voice trembled when she asked the question, and Griffin moved toward her. She'd been hurt earlier, and he hadn't had the chance to assess how badly.

"Why what?"

Joseph's voice was nothing like Griffin remembered. It was rough and hateful. Cold, like it was missing something. Could turning into the killer he'd become have robbed him of some aspect of his humanity? Griffin didn't know, but hearing Joseph talk gave him the chills. He wanted to get the man as far away from him as possible, but they weren't quite done yet.

"Why did you kill them?"

Her voice was insistent but fragile. She must have realized, as he had, that it would take something incredible for Addy to be alive at this point.

"I was hunting."

Griffin wanted to throw up. The man continued to talk, explaining that when he'd shot Megan, it had been an accident. He'd thought she was a bear on the mountainside. When he'd realized he'd shot a person, he had panicked and triggered the avalanche to cover up what he'd done.

Like he'd been hit, Griffin flinched when he'd mentioned the avalanche. Bre met his eyes. All these years he'd blamed himself…the technicians and investigators had determined that the avalanche had been human triggered, remotely, but that hadn't meant Griffin had done it.

He'd wasted years of his life feeling guilty about something he hadn't even done. While it was true that Griffin hadn't handled that search perfectly, he also hadn't made costly mistakes that had cost someone a life, something he'd believed for far too long. The relief and the unfairness of it made him want to weep.

"After I shot her... I couldn't... I had to—" He broke off.

"Had to what?"

He wouldn't say any more, but the answer seemed clear to Griffin. He'd had to keep hunting, and reenacting the murder he hadn't meant to commit by committing one after another up in the mountain passes. Hunting women the way he'd once hunted animals, disposing of their bodies in sites where he'd once helped rescue people and save their lives, bringing it all into a disturbing full circle.

Stomach churning, Griffin was fairly sure he was going to be sick.

"And Addy? She was someone you know, or at least had to have recognized after working with me before. Why my niece?"

Refusing to break, Joseph just shook his head, eyes focused somewhere past them in the distance. Finally, he said. "She came into the pass. I hunted her."

If there'd been any hope he hadn't gotten to her, that ended it. Griffin's heart sank to his stomach and this time he did have to turn and vomit. Embarrassed, he looked at Bre. Her eyes were red, tears streaming down her face, but her determined expression made her look stronger than he'd ever seen her.

"And where *is she*?"

"Where. Is. My. Niece?" She moved a step closer.

Joseph swung his legs, tried to trip her and bring her down, but Griffin pulled her back and into his arms.

"Easy, Bre," he whispered in her ear. "He won't help you, but he will kill you if he can. Don't get any closer."

Now her sobs broke loose. He moved her as she cried, and they embraced, so that he was between her and the killer, confident that nothing was going to happen to her. Not able to do anything else, he just held her while she wept for Addy.

And probably for all the others. For them. For what had been lost because of one person's evil.

The noise of the chopper the chief had sent was a welcome relief. It was over. Mostly. They still needed to find Addy's body, to find closure for Bre, and to give her some sense of this nightmare ending, though in some ways Griffin knew that it was only beginning.

If she'd let him, though, he would be there for her. He didn't want to be at all like the man on the ground before him, defined by one mistake. Griffin had lost enough time thinking he wasn't capable or worthy and, if Bre would take him back again, he would spend every minute of his life not bemoaning the fact that he wasn't good enough for her. Instead, he'd spend that time proving he would put in the work to be good enough for her.

Because life was short. Heartbreakingly so for some people, like Addy, but every moment of it was a gift. Griffin was tired of half living it.

The police wasted no time in climbing out of the helicopter and taking custody of Joseph. The chief had come along and walked up to Griffin and Bre to address them before talking to the man in the handcuffs.

"This him?"

Griffin stayed quiet, knowing this was Bre's case to

wrap up. While she talked, he petted his dogs, both of which were sitting at his feet.

"Yes. It's him. You were right. First responder."

"Joseph?"

Bre and Griffin nodded.

"Prints from your mudroom came back just before I flew out as belonging to him. We should have a good case against him. And a search-and-rescue worker… the FBI was right. I guess it is good we brought them in and I guess their new methods work okay."

Bre was grinning. Griffin had worked with the chief enough to know that what he'd said was high praise, even if his voice was gruff.

"We'll take him in. And then send another copter for you and Addy, to get you to the hospital." His eyes were on Bre's shoulder. "You need to get that looked at."

"I will. I just need a minute to look around. Think. Maybe pray."

The chief seemed to understand the way the situation had changed, the fact that Bre had finally lost her hope of finding Addy alive. It was over, but not the way any of them had hoped it would have ended.

"Take your minute. But when the chopper gets here, I want you on it. You need a doctor."

Griffin tended to agree. Her face was growing paler. He'd thought it was emotion, but the way she was clutching that arm told him it hurt more than he'd realized. No wonder. The arrow had gone entirely through, tearing a massive hole in the back most likely.

"Sounds good." Bre walked toward the cabin and Griffin followed her, reaching around to put his arm behind her and rub her upper back.

"I'm sorry about how all of this worked out. I'm sorry about Addy."

"Nothing you could have done. We did all we could." She looked out into the distance. "But she was up here, you think?"

"The dogs think so."

She'd forgotten about the animals, it seemed like, from the surprised look on her face. When he followed her gaze to the huskies at his feet, he realized they weren't there anymore.

Barking behind them caught his attention. Incessant noise. And then a howl.

Shivers chased down his spine. Closure was going to come sooner than he'd anticipated, whether they were ready or not.

The dogs had found her.

SEVENTEEN

It was funny how a person could be sure they couldn't hurt worse and then something else could cause the pain to stab deeper, like a knife that just kept digging. Bre had been sure her heart would break so many times in the last few days, but this time she knew it was true. The dogs had found Addy's body.

Bre was out of breath when she tried to walk, and the dizziness hadn't improved, but she owed it to Addy to see this through. As she moved as quickly as she could to the spot where the dogs had alerted, she squinted against the brightness of the sun, offended somehow that such a gorgeous day could be full of so much sadness and injustice. Someone had ruined it by bringing evil into it.

She guessed it was like life. Maybe God didn't want evil to happen. He'd made the world, yet it had turned against Him and chosen its own way instead. Broken what should have been a perfect picture.

Maybe days like today broke God's heart even more than they broke hers. It was His creation who was being killed, devastated.

Never had Bre considered that God could be hurt by

people's bad choices. But if He hurt a fraction of how much she did right now, it wouldn't surprise her. Probably, He hurt even worse.

"What is this?" Bre asked Griffin when she came to where the dogs were.

"Root cellar. These homesteader cabins sometimes had root cellars and smokehouses."

She swallowed hard. "Is she…?"

"Their alert was confusing. I don't know. It sounded like they were alerting to…" He shook his head and Bre heard his voice break. "I don't know what we are going to find. Do you want me to look first? Then I can—"

"No," she answered before he finished speaking, biting the word out among the pain, physical and emotional. "I will look. But I can't move the door."

Griffin shoved the lid aside, scraping it against the dirt and dust, which scattered in the air.

Bre held her breath and leaned over the edge.

There she was, wearing the same outfit she'd disappeared in. Looking small. Fragile. Beautiful. But broken. Her clothes were bloodstained.

Bre caught a sob in her throat and just stared, emotions threatening to overwhelm her…

Then she blinked as she took in her niece's crumped form.

Up…down…up…down…

Addy was breathing.

"Griffin!" He'd stepped back, maybe to give her privacy in such a hard moment, Bre didn't know, but he was thankfully still close. Her vision was fogging and her arm hurt so badly she knew she didn't have long before the injury made her pass out, but she had to see this through first. "She is breathing!"

And then he was right there, like he'd been this entire search process, bending and pulling Addy out.

Bre kept watching, eyes starving for the sight of her niece. She kept tabs on her breaths, just to make sure it hadn't been wishful thinking, but Addy was very definitely breathing. She was pale, her dark blond hair tangled, her clothes matted with dirt and what looked like blood, but she looked so very beautiful to Bre. So very alive.

"Sweet girl." She brushed a hand along Addy's cheek and Addy sighed.

Her lips moved but no sound came out.

"Shh-hhh, it's okay," Bre said, blinking back more tears. "It's going to be okay."

Addy was in rough shape, but she was alive, and that more than anything else gave Bre the hope to believe that she might truly be okay. Maybe God was showing her something. That sometimes people left her. Sometimes His answer to her request would be no, like it had been when she'd begged beside her bed on the floor as a faith-filled child to have her mom back out of jail.

But sometimes the answer would be yes. Sometimes everything worked out, even on earth.

Sometimes hope really did overpower the darkness. Even when the darkness was very, very dark.

"You came." Addy's whisper was loud enough to be heard this time.

"Of course I did, sweet girl."

"Dad said you would always be there for me..." Her words trailed off. "He said you would. And God told me you'd come..."

"I believe in Him now too. I know He helped us find you."

Addy's lips quivered as she tried to smile.

"What happened, Addy?" Bre caught herself. "Or we can talk about it later."

"I'll tell you now what I can…so tired…thirsty. I don't think I've had water in a couple of days. I know that's really bad, that's what you taught me…" she choked out.

Bre saw Griffin out of the corner of her eye, digging in his backpack for a water bottle.

They offered it to Addy. She drank a couple sips slowly and then blinked her eyes. "Thanks." The sun was bright and she squinted. "Are these your dogs, Griffin?"

"Meet Flapjack and Ember." Bre introduced them. "They are the ones who found you."

"Seriously? That's really cool. I thought I heard them barking one night, the first night I was out in the pass after I got shot the first time."

"The first time?" Griffin asked, and Bre tried to take deep breaths. She couldn't imagine her being shot at all, much less twice. Bre knew how awful that was and hated that Addy had had to experience that.

The water seemed to have helped her gain a little more strength because her voice sounded a little stronger now. "I was hiking and he shot me, but I managed to get away. I tried to get back to somewhere you could find me, since I knew you'd be looking, but every time I thought I was safe, he got close again and started shooting. Finally, he hit me again and that time I couldn't… I just couldn't run anymore. He brought me here and left me. I thought he'd left me to die."

Bre didn't correct her, but she suspected Addy's assumption had been right. Her first impression was not that Joseph had been living in the cabin. It seemed more like the other sites where bodies had been located, where there was just a connection to a search-and-rescue case he'd worked. More than likely, he'd been sticking close to make sure that Addy died before anyone found her, and to ensure he was able to kill anyone who came close.

The rumble of the second chopper as it approached was the second-best noise Bre had heard today, second only to Addy's sweet voice.

"I'm so glad you're alive," Bre said over the growing cacophony.

"Me too. I'm sorry I came out here."

"How did you get out here?" Bre was yelling now to be heard, and Addy probably couldn't talk that loudly, so she shook her head.

EMTs poured from the chopper and Bre and Griffin helped them settle Addy onto a stretcher.

She reached for Bre right before they loaded her in the helicopter. "He brought me out here. He told me something had happened to you and I needed to come immediately. I said I'd drive, but he thought I would be too upset…" She paused. "It sounds stupid now and exactly like a setup. But I thought…"

Bre knew how she thought. When you got used to losing people, it made sense in your head that you would keep losing people. It was obvious that she'd struggled with that in her own life. It pained her to imagine Addy had, too, and that she hadn't felt able to address it with her aunt.

"It's okay. You're okay."

One more wave of nausea washed through Bre and the blackness started to close over her.

"You'd better go too," Griffin encouraged her.

She'd better go. He wasn't coming? Maybe she'd misread his look earlier, but she'd really thought... She'd hoped...

An EMT reached out to steady her and Bre let him catch her. She couldn't hold her own weight anymore.

"You're going to be okay," he reassured her, much like she'd just reassured Addy.

They loaded into the helicopter and Bre couldn't help but notice that Griffin didn't follow.

"You're not coming?" Bre asked even though she knew she shouldn't. But she had to know.

He shook his head. He started to say something as Bre looked away. She didn't have the strength to hear whatever he had to say right now. She had to focus on Addy and on getting well.

They'd only started to lift off when her eyes closed and she could no longer focus on anything at all.

Back in a hospital again, Griffin tried not to let the sterile environment get to him. The atmosphere might not be his favorite, but this time it was hard to hate the hospital too much. The two women he cared about most in the world were on their way to recovery because of the work of people in this facility.

And because of God. Griffin was thankful, so thankful. How easily this story could have had a different ending, and it hadn't. God had stepped in at the last minute when he'd been so sure it was too late.

Maybe it was never too late for God. Bre certainly seemed to have found Him, from what she'd said to Addy, and he hadn't stopped thanking God for it. She shared his faith now, and Addy was alive. He couldn't have asked for more.

Griffin sighed as he left Addy's room. Twenty-four hours had passed since they'd been brought to the hospital. Both of them had been in worse shape than anticipated, according to the nurse he'd talked to. Technically speaking, they couldn't give him any information since he wasn't family, but one particular nurse looked like she was about eighty and couldn't care less about privacy rules. He'd never been so thankful for someone raised before the internet and privacy regulations. Still, he wanted to see them in person, but doctors had cautioned it might be too much for the first day.

That was why he had spent almost all that time in the hospital waiting room. He wanted to be close and that had been the best he could do.

Now that he was able to visit them, he'd gone to see Addy first, feeling like it was appropriate to speak to one of Bre's relatives before he asked the question he was about to ask. As he'd suspected, she'd given him a hard time for not pursuing Bre years ago and given her wholehearted approval of Griffin asking Bre to marry him.

"Just make sure not to schedule the wedding till I'm out of the hospital."

"You should be out next week," he'd said dryly. "I don't think we're in *that* big of a hurry."

"After the years you guys have waited to finally admit that you both love each other? I wouldn't be surprised if you managed to find someone here to marry you before you left the building. But that's not romantic, and I want to be there, so like I said, you have to wait till I'm out of the hospital."

"Deal." They'd shaken on it.

Now he was walking down the hall to Bre's room.

He knocked on the door, wondering if a man ever got used to the feeling of wearing his heart on his sleeve. After all their stops and starts, was what he was asking too much?

On the other hand, Addy was right. He should have done this years ago.

"Come in," she called.

"How are you feeling?" he asked as he opened the door.

"Griffin!" Her voice was surprised. He moved into the room just as she scooted up in the bed, her back against the propped-up pillows she was using as a backrest. She was slightly paler than usual, which made her dark eyes look even darker, and her blond hair fell softly around her shoulders. "You're here."

"Of course I'm here."

"You didn't come on the helicopter ride, so I thought…" She let her words fall off, then seemed to sit straighter and continued. "I wanted to talk to you and tell you about how God didn't give up on me and I believe now… But you weren't here, I thought I'd just talk to you sometime later."

Griffin's eyebrows raised. He stepped closer. "That is something I'm so thankful to hear. He never gives up on us."

"No, He doesn't. And He never leaves us alone."

"He doesn't, but even knowing He's with you doesn't stop me from wanting to be here too, if you don't mind my company? You don't sound like you'd expected it."

"It's not that I didn't want you here, but I thought you might not want to be here. I know you don't like hospitals."

How had she known that about him? Then again, he

shouldn't be surprised. He probably knew things about her that she didn't know he knew, as many years as they'd been watching each other and getting to know one another. And as many years as they'd loved one another...

"I wanted to come on the helicopter. But they wouldn't let me. It's against policy. Even when I got here, they said with the extent of your injuries I should wait twenty-four hours."

Bre glanced at the clock on the wall. "Twenty-four hours and...what, like twenty or thirty minutes?"

"Well, I had to talk to Addy first."

"How is she? They keep telling me she's fine, but it's not the same as seeing her."

"She seems great. You're not the least bit curious why I had to talk to her before I talked to you?"

"No, I..." Bre hesitated. "Wait, you talked to her first? What about?"

Her voice was light, but she was suspicious, Griffin could tell.

"About this." He pulled the ring out of his pocket, moved toward the bed, and went down on one knee on the hospital floor. "I love you, Bre Dayton. I've made a huge mess of things so many times, I wouldn't blame you if you told me I was out of chances. But I have loved you for years and I will love you for years to come, and I would love to marry you and keep on loving you forever."

For the second time in as many days, he saw her eyes fill with tears. Bre, who rarely cried. Maybe it was good, though; maybe God was healing some of her old hurts, washing the wounds with the salty tears so that they would heal properly.

"So, are you asking me something?" she said with a smile through the tears.

"You're right. I haven't technically asked anything…" He reached for her hand and lifted it gently into his, rubbing his thumb along her smooth skin. "Will you marry me, Bre? Please?"

A grin bigger than any he could ever remember seeing spread across her face and she laughed.

"I would love to marry you. I love you so much." She reached her arms out and Griffin stood and moved closer. She pulled him into a hug and squeezed him tight. When they parted, he slid a ring out of his pocket, and then slid it onto her finger. It was a perfect fit, even though, when he'd bought it at the jewelry store yesterday, he'd told them he'd take his chances with the size and fix it later if it didn't fit. But it did.

Almost like it was meant to be.

"I would marry you right now," she admitted. "Right now, like this, just to be with you. That's how much I love you."

Now it was his turn to laugh. "Your niece made me promise I'd wait till we were out of the hospital."

"Speaking of my niece, that's not her is it?"

Griffin turned around to face the door.

"Did I miss it?" Addy was in a wheelchair, at the entrance to the hospital room, grinning.

"We're getting married." Bre laughed and held up her hand, where his ring sparkled like all his dreams were coming true.

Griffin could hear the smile in Bre's voice, could see it on her face, and it made him feel more at peace than he'd ever felt.

"Ahhh!" Addy squealed and rolled the chair into the

room. "When? Am I the maid of honor? We could do it today!"

"You're the one who said we had to wait till you were out of the hospital."

"I don't care, I just can't believe we're going to be a family."

A family. Maybe they'd always been something of a family, but they were going to make it official.

Griffin liked the sound of that.

"Aren't you supposed to kiss after you officially get engaged?"

He liked the sound of that too. So kiss her he did.

* * * * *

Dear Reader,

Thanks so much for coming along for another Alaskan adventure! I loved getting to tell Bre and Griffin's story, and I especially enjoyed including several of my favorite things—the Alaskan wilderness and dogs—in the story.

Bre and Griffin both struggle with different issues in this book, different lies they believe that are hurting their lives and relationships. Bre believes that people always leave, since she's experienced that in life so much, and it takes time for her to learn to trust God and to trust people too. Griffin's struggles are more against himself; he doesn't believe he is worthy of Bre or her love, and needs to see himself the way God sees him. Both characters have struggles that are common to many people. If these are issues that have come up in your own life, I hope you feel like you can talk to God about them, or to some trusted people in your life, and continue to let God's truth replace any lies you believe.

As far as the Alaskan wilderness, some details have been fictionalized and changed, in this fictional story. For example, Wolf River is not a real town. But the Alaskan wilderness is an amazing place that needs no exaggeration. I highly recommend adventuring in South Central Alaska, if you have the chance, especially near the Chugach Mountains, and enjoying some of the same scenery Bre and Griffin saw in this story.

As a last fun note, Alaskan huskies, the type of dog featured in this story, are a special type of dog that is extra special to me as I own several. To see photos of my huskies, follow me on Instagram (@sarahvarland) or on Facebook (@sarahvarlandauthor).

I love hearing from my readers! Feel free to email me, sarahvarland@gmail.com if you'd like to say hi. Thank you again for reading. I love getting to tell stories and I hope you have as much fun reading them as I do writing them.

Sarah Varland

ALASKAN AVALANCHE ESCAPE
K-9 Search and Rescue • by Darlene L. Turner
After discovering someone is deliberately triggering avalanches, mountain survival expert Jayla Hoyt and her K-9 set out to stop the culprit—but he sets his sights on them. Can she and Alaska park ranger Bryson Clarke catch the criminal before they all lose their lives?

GUARDING HIS CHILD
by Karen Kirst
Following her best friend's gruesome murder, Deputy Skye Saddler is assigned to protect the victim's baby and the father who didn't know the little girl existed. Now that rancher Nash Wilder is the killer's next target, keeping close to Skye is their best chance at survival.

DETECTING SECRETS
Deputies of Anderson County • by Sami A. Abrams
When pregnant teens and babies go missing, Sheriff Dennis Monroe works with marriage and family therapist Charlotte Bradley and her air-scent dog to put an end to a black-market baby smuggling ring in Anderson County. But when the kidnapper's scheme includes Charlotte, can she rely on Dennis to protect her?

PERILOUS SECURITY DETAIL
Honor Protection Specialists • by Elizabeth Goddard
When bodyguard Everly Honor rescues her secretive ex-boyfriend from an intentional hit-and-run, he hires her to guard his niece. But with danger closing in on all sides, Sawyer Blackwood must reveal hidden truths...or put their lives at risk.

DEADLY VENGEANCE
by Jodie Bailey
Someone wants profiler Gabe Buchanan dead, and he has no idea why. When his identity is wiped clean, he's forced to trust military investigator Hannah Austin, the woman who hurt him in the past, to restore his life. As deadly threats escalate, they'll have to find the culprit before it's too late.

THEME PARK ABDUCTION
by Patsy Conway
A cartel kidnaps Rebecca Salmon's son off a roller coaster, and now she needs help from FBI agent Jake Foster to solve a series of clues planted throughout the theme park. As they race against time and evade henchmen gunning for them, will Jake's secrets get in the way of saving her son?

LISCNM0123

HARLEQUIN
PLUS

Announcing a **BRAND-NEW** multimedia subscription service for romance fans like you!

Read, Watch and Play.

Experience the easiest way to get the romance content you crave.

Start your **FREE 7 DAY TRIAL** at <u>www.harlequinplus.com/freetrial</u>.